TIED TO A BOSS 5

J. L. ROSE

Good2Go Publishing

TIED TO A BOSS 5
Written by J. L. Rose
Cover Design: Davida Baldwin
Typesetter: Mychea
ISBN: 9781947340008
Copyright ©2017 Good2Go Publishing
Published 2017 by Good2Go Publishing
7311 W. Glass Lane • Laveen, AZ 85339
www.good2gopublishing.com
https://twitter.com/good2gobooks
G2G@good2gopublishing.com
www.facebook.com/good2gopublishing
www.instagram.com/good2gopublishing

ACKNOWLEDGEMENTS

To my Heavenly Father, thanks for always holding me down, and also to my fans. I love each and every one of you who picks up one of my novels and takes these rides I put together for each of you. Thank you all! Peace!

DEDICATION

This book is for the one person who believed in me without meeting me and only read my letter asking for a chance. To my boy, Ray Brown. Thanks for everything!

TIED TO A BOSS 5

PROLOGUE

Once the family was all crowded inside the front room of his suite—minus Tony T, Dre, James, Kyree, and Gage, who were out handling business—Dante briefly explained to them the problem they were facing. He then let everyone know there was a traitor among the family.

"Who?" Vanessa asked, with her face balled up in anger.

"How do you know all this, fam?" Floyd asked as he and his team stood off to the side together.

"I'ma show you all proof, but if anyone reacts, I will deal with them myself." Dante worried as he handed over his phone to Alinna.

She, in turn, handed the phone to Yasmine on her left and told her to look through the pictures.

While waiting for the phone to make its way back to him as each family member looked at the photos, Dante began to hear mumbling. He then heard the front door open just as Dre and Tony walked inside.

"What's going on in here?" Dre asked, looking around the

room and seeing confused faces and pissed-off looks. He noticed the cell phone being passed around and said, "What's going on, fam?"

"Come here, Andre!" Vanessa told her man.

Harmony walked over to Tony T, grabbed his hand, and led him over to where she was sitting.

"What the fuck is this?" Maxine yelled, after looking at the pictures on the phone. "This is bullshit, Dante! These pictures don't mean a fucking thing!"

"Fuck that shit, Alinna! These pictures don't mean shit!" Maxine yelled, after Alinna asked her to relax.

"You feel that way?" Dante spoke up, drawing everyone in the room's attention to him.

"Once he gets here, we'll see just how true these pictures are. And since you want to be the spokesperson, you'll also be the one to deal with this problem."

"Dante, that's not right!" Keisha spoke up, standing beside her sister just as the front door opened again and in walked James, Gage, and Kyree.

"What's going on up in here?" James asked, looking around at the expressions on everyone's faces.

"Gage!" Dante spoke up. "Close the door, and if anybody gets close to the door before we're done here, kill 'em!"

"Not a problem, boss!" Gage replied, closing the front door and then pulling out his banger and positioning himself in front of the now-locked door.

"Maxine, come here!" Dante demanded.

Dante handed Maxine his banger when she walked over to him, and then he told James to let Kyree see the pictures.

"We now have everyone here. Now, let's see if what we've all seen is the truth or a lie! It's on you, Maxine. Handle your business, shorty," Dante instructed.

ONE

"Whoa!" Kyree cried, after seeing the pictures that were on the cell phone that James had just handed him, and now understanding why everybody was staring at him crazy-like. "Dante, man! This is not what it looks like!"

"It's not, huh?" Dante asked him, leaning back against the wall and folding his arms across his chest. "From what I seen and what the family's seen, it looks like you and this punk-ass clown Fish Man together. Why's that?"

"Let me explain, Dante!" Kyree begged, noticing the gun in Maxine's hands for the first time.

"I'm listening!" Dante told him.

Taking a deep breath and trying to calm himself a little, Kyree started explaining: "It's like this. This dude I was doing business with back in Miami named Gator was out here with his new business partner, and dude got at me earlier today. But when I told him I was out here we hooked up. He wanted me to meet his partner, and that's how I ran into Fish Man. He remembered me and we talked, but I've got him believing that I don't fuck with the family no more. I was going to tell you when I walked inside here, but all this jumped off when I stepped foot in here. I swear that's the truth. I ain't got no reason to betray the family."

Dante listened to what Kyree had to say, and stared at the boy a few moments. He then looked over to Alinna on his left and was surprised to see her nod her head at him.

"I believe you, Kyree. You said Fish Man thinks you're no longer with us, right?" Alinna said directly to him.

"That's what I told him!" Kyree admitted.

Nodding her head as she began thinking, Alinna then said, "Okay, this is what you're going to do, Kyree! You're going to lay this whole thing out! I want you to continue meeting with Fish Man and earn his trust. Try to become a part of his organization, but I want you to report directly back to me every Friday. Are we understood, Kyree?"

"Perfectly!" Kyree answered, but then said, "It shouldn't be hard getting a position with Fish Man since he already offered me a spot on his team."

"Dante!" Alinna called out to him, getting her husband's

attention. "Please give me your car keys!"

Dante stared at Alinna a brief moment but dug out his new Audi keys. He then walked over to his wife and handed over his keys to her.

Alinna thanked her husband, only to turn and toss the keys to Kyree.

"The car is yours. If you're going to play the part of a boss, you need to drive like the boss! Remember what I said, Kyree. Do not make me look like the fool!" Alinna said.

"I got you, Alinna! That's my word on my life!" he told her in all honesty.

"I plan on holding you to that exact promise," Dante spoke up.

* * *

After ending the meeting a few minutes later and releasing Kyree, Dante waited until everyone left but Yasmine, Natalie, Gage, and James. He then looked over at Alinna still in her seat and stared straight at her. "Explain, Alinna!" he demanded.

"Is there really a reason to?" Alinna asked him. "I explained everything while everyone was still here, and you heard everything that was said, Dante."

"So you actually believe the story that boy gave us?"

"Yes, I do!"

"I do as well, Dante," Natalie spoke up, agreeing with Alinna.

"My husband, I'm sorry. But I believe him as well," Yasmine added as she met her husband's eyes.

Dante shook his head and actually chuckled as he looked over at each of his three wives. He sighed and said, "Alright. I trust the three of you, so I'll go along with this whole thing because it's what you three want."

"Thank you," Alinna told her husband, smiling at him. "And don't worry about the new car. We'll buy you another one."

Dante shook his head just as his phone rang. He dug out his cell phone to see that his mother was calling him.

"Yeah, Momma. Everything alright?"

"Yes, baby. I'm just calling to give you the number to your contact guy that Patrick just gave me."

"What's the number?" Dante asked while programming the number in his mind as his mother called it out to him.

"His name is Aaron Howard, Dante! He's a lieutenant

detective."

"Thanks, Momma."

"Are you coming over for dinner tonight?"

"I'll be there."

Dante hung up the phone with his mother with a smile and then looked up to find everyone staring at him.

"What I do?" he asked, causing everybody to burst out laughing at him.

* * *

"James, we need to talk!" Mari announced, catching James inside the hallway after leaving Dante, Alinna, Yasmine, Natalie, and the others' suite.

She walked right up on James and with her hands on her hips asked, "When was you planning on telling me about this Maxine woman?"

James heard the elevator and looked back down the hall, only to see Natalie's bodyguards and friend walk off the elevator, arms full with Rose, Emmy, and the kids. He then nodded to Gomez and even bent down to hug a smiling Mya.

"Hi, James!" Rose said, receiving a kiss on the cheek from him.

"James!"

James recognized the voice that yelled out his name, and he looked back to see Maxine heading his way. He didn't even hear the elevator arrive, but he fully recognized the expression on Maxine's face.

"I know you're not out here with this bitch!" Maxine yelled as she stopped beside James and snatched him around to face her. "You're really going to get this bitch hurt if you don't keep her out of your face!"

"You're not doing anything to me, bitch!" Mari yelled, only for Maxine to take off a second later, rushing at her.

"Fuck!" James yelled, rushing at both Mari and Maxine as the two of them went at each other.

He was surprised Mari was actually throwing some pretty good blows, but she really wasn't a match for Maxine.

"Break this shit up!" Dante yelled as he, Gage, and Gomez rushed out of the suite after hearing the commotion in the hall.

Dante got both women apart, only for Maxine to rush back toward Mari and attempt another swing. Gomez stepped in front of Mari and took the blow that was thrown for Maxine.

"That's enough!" Dante yelled. His voice caused every-

6

body to freeze and stare straight at him. "I swear to God! The next person who swings, I will send them to the hospital's intensive care unit! Try me! Please, try me!" he continued.

Dante then looked back and forth between Maxine and Mari and saw that neither woman wanted to move. He then looked over at James.

"Bruh, you need to handle this shit! I'm serious! Fix this shit or let them both go!" Dante said.

"I got it!" James stated angrily, but then surprised both Maxine and Mari and started yelling "Let's go now!"

Dante watched as both Mari and Maxine followed behind a pissed off James. Dante shook his head as he turned and headed back to his suite with Gage and Gomez behind him.

TWO

Dante heard the sliding glass door open up behind him while standing out on the balcony smoking one of his Black & Milds and thinking. He looked back over his right shoulder to see Alinna step out into the balcony with him.

"Hey, you!" Alinna said as she walked up beside her husband. "What's up?"

"Just thinking about something my mom told me," Dante admitted. "What's good though?"

"I was talking with Yasmine and Natalie, and they want to find a place out of Syracuse if we're staying in New York."

"Where?"

"Buffalo, New York."

Dante looked over to Alinna, met her eyes, shook his head, and then focused his attention back out over the city.

"Go ahead and get it done, but while you're doing that, also find a spot for my mom and Dwayne. I wanna get her out of Syracuse."

Dante and Alinna heard the sliding glass door open again.

As they turned around they saw Natalie step out onto the balcony.

"Baby, your mother's on the phone!" Natalie told Dante, handing him his cell phone.

Dante thanked his wife as he took the phone from her. He then placed the phone up to his ear.

"Yeah, Momma. What's up? You okay?"

"I'm fine, sweetheart. But can you come back to the house for a minute, please?"

"I'm on my way," Dante told his mother, already moving toward the sliding glass door.

As he hung up the phone, both Alinna and Natalie were behind him questioning him if everything was alright.

* * *

Dante left the hotel with Gage, James, Tony T, and Dre. They made it back out to his mother's place only to see a navy-blue Jaguar XK convertible parked out in front of her house, along with her husband Dwayne's truck. Dante was the first one out of the Escalade, followed by James and then Dre. He headed up to the front door and knocked.

"Hey, sweetheart!" Brenda said, smiling and accepting the

kiss from Dante after opening the front door to find her son. "Come on inside. There's someone here that wants to meet you."

"Excuse me, Momma Blackwell," James said as first he and then Gage entered the house before Dante.

Brenda shook her head and smiled at seeing how loyal and protective her son's friends were of him. She then took her son's arm and led him into the house as Dre and Tony T followed him inside. She escorted Dante into the front room where a white female with straight, long, black hair in a ponytail was sitting on the sofa with Dwayne across from her.

"Lieutenant Megan Lewis, this is my son."

"Dante Blackwell!" Lieutenant Lewis finished for Brenda while staring up at the legendary bad boy himself.

She was more shocked and surprised at how breathtakingly handsome he was as she stood up and held out her hand to him.

"Mom, who's this?" Dante asked, ignoring the woman's hand while staring straight into her emerald green eyes.

"I was assigned to you by Chief Grant," Lieutenant Lewis spoke up, answering Dante's question. "I'm supposed to watch your back. Well, watch it in other areas, since it seems you have enough people watching your back as it is!"

Dante nodded his head slowly after what he was just told. He then looked over at his mother and saw her smile of approval. He looked back at Lewis.

"You ready to get to work?"

"That's what I'm being paid to do!" she told Dante, pulling out a writing pad and paper, only for Dante to shake his head.

"No notes! I don't believe in writing anything down that can lead back to me! Everything is stored in the mind, so start getting used to it!"

Lewis was impressed and nodded her head as she put away her writing pad and pen.

"Okay, Blackwell. What you need?" she asked.

"First, I need you to find out all the information you can about an Antonio Mitchell, and I want to know everything you can find out about a Garcia something."

"Francisco!" Lieutenant Lewis stated, but saw the look on Dante's face. "That's Garcia's name—Garcia Francisco. And it won't be hard gathering information on him. I can have that for you by tonight, but I'll get on finding out about this Antonio Mitchell for you. Is there anything else you need?"

"Not at the moment," Dante answered.

"Well, here's my card," she told Dante, handing over a black card. "My cell number is in gold. Call it whenever. It doesn't matter what time of the day."

Dante took the card and nodded his thanks. He then sat down on the sofa as his mother walked the lieutenant to the door. He looked over toward Dwayne, who was reading the newspaper.

"Dwayne, let me talk to you a second."

"What's up, son?" Dwayne asked as he folded up the newspaper and laid it on top of the coffee table.

Dante then looked up as his mother re-entered the room and sat down beside him.

"Mom, I was just about to talk to Dwayne, but I want to talk to you too," Dante said as he looked at both of them.

"What's the matter, sweetheart?" Brenda asked with a concerned look on her face.

"Relax, Momma," Dante began, noting the look on her face. "It's nothing bad. I just wanna ask a favor from the two of you."

"What is it, sweety?"

"I want to buy you and Dwayne a new house. I want to move the two of you out of Syracuse and to Buffalo where Alinna wants to move the family."

"Dante, are you serious?" Brenda asked her son in disbelief. "Baby, that's going to cost a lot of money to move all of us out there."

"Mom," Dante stated, smirking at his mother, "money isn't an issue. Believe me. Just tell me you'll move."

"What about Dwayne's job and my work, Dante?" Brenda asked.

"I tell you what," Dante started as he began smiling, "how about the two of you find a business you want or begin your own business, and I'll pay for it?"

"Dante, are you serious?" Brenda asked her son, looking over to her husband who sat quietly watching her son. "Dwayne, honey! What do you think?"

"What do you want to do?" Dwayne asked his wife. "I'm all for whatever makes you happy, and who am I to turn down an offer like this one Dante's offering us?"

Brenda broke into a big smile and turned back toward her son. "When can we begin looking around for houses?" she asked.

"We can go as soon as Alinna contacts a real estate agent," Dante told his mother, just as the front door opened, drawing everyone's attention.

"Dante!" Melody cried out happily as she and her boyfriend entered the house. "What are you doing here?"

"Momma called me," Dante answered while staring at the guy with his sister. "Who's homeboy you with?"

"Dante, this is my boyfriend, Norise!" Melody told her brother and then introduced Norise to him.

"Boyfriend, huh?" Dante stated as he stood up from his seat, only to have his phone begin to ring from inside his pocket. He dug out the phone while staring at Norise.

"Yeah!"

"Dante, it's Floyd, Cuz."

"Yeah! What's good, Cuzo?"

"You still wanna get a look around the spots like we spoke about?"

"Yeah! Where you at?"

"I'm out at Brooklyn Park now. You wanna come through, or do you want me to come to you?"

14

"Naw! I'm on my way now," Dante told Floyd before hanging up the phone.

Dante then looked over at Norise and said, "We'll talk later, boyfriend. We will talk later."

"Dante, are you coming back for dinner tonight, baby?" Brenda asked as she stood up and began walking her son to the front door.

"I'll be back, mom," Dante told her, kissing his mother's cheek before following his boys from the house.

* * *

Dante left his mother's house and drove over to Brooklyn Park. There he spotted Floyd, Nina, Beast, and the twins, Kaos and Corrupt, standing beside a Lincoln Navigator. Dante then let down his window as Gage pulled up behind the Navigator.

"What's up, Cuz?" Floyd called out when he saw Dante, walking over to the Escalade passenger window. "You ready to go?"

"We'll follow you, Cuzo," Dante told his cousin before he let back up his window as Floyd walked back over to his team.

Dante left Brooklyn Park and followed behind the Navigator into which Floyd and his crew climbed. He then gc a look around the city and saw the different spots that were being worked by different hustlers. Dante watched the Navigator as it pulled to a stop in front of a Quickie Mart that looked surprisingly busy, even with the five guys that hung out around the front of the store.

"Here comes your cousin," Gage told Dante, seeing Floyd climb from the SUV and then start in the direction of the Escalade.

Dante let down his window as Floyd walked up.

"What's good, Cuzo? What's this spot right here?" Dante asked.

"This is the spot I told you about that I was fucking with until those niggas Gator and Fish Man saw how busy this shit be and put a team out here to get money."

"So that's the team right there?" Dante asked, nodding over to the five guys positioned out in front of the store.

"Yeah!" Floyd answered as he nodded across the street and nodded again toward the end of the block on the corner. "There are two more. One's across the street, and another one is on the corner on the right from us."

Dante slowly nodded his head and then called out to Dre in

the back of the Escalade.

"What's up, fam?" Dre answered as he sat forward between the two front seats.

"Fam, you and Tony T go up there with Floyd. But I'm sure y'all know what's up, right?" Dante asked his brother.

"About time we get to have some fun!" Dre stated as he and Tony T climbed from the Escalade.

Dante watched as Floyd walked toward the five guys up to the front of the store, with Dre on his left and Tony T on his right.

"Take care of the two lookouts!" Dante called to James.

* * *

"If it ain't lil' man, Floyd!" Tank stated, smiling as Floyd walked up in front of him and then noticing two unknown faces. "I see you brought new friends with you. What you want out on this end?"

"I'ma make this quick, son," Floyd told Tank. "This spot right here is under new management from this moment on. You and ya boys can leave or get carried off. What's it gonna be?"

Tank laughed in Floyd's face after hearing what he had to say. He then looked to his right at his boy, nodding to Floyd.

He looked back at Floyd only to freeze and instantly lose his smile as he stared down the barrel of a chrome .45 automatic.

"Maybe you thought my little cousin was playing about what the fuck he just said!" Dre stated in a calm voice. "So let me make this shit clear. It's over with. So as of right now, I'ma need you and the rest of ya boys to get naked, just like you dropped out of the pussy, and lay the fuck down on the ground!"

After seeing Tank look past him on his right, Dre smirked and nodded to his left.

"Looking for those two right there?" he asked.

Tank looked to his far right, only to see a white boy holding both his backup men at gunpoint on their knees with their hand behind their heads.

"Who the fuck is you niggas?" Tank looked back and asked Dre.

"Just tell ya boss, Fish Man, that his old friend from Miami says, 'What's up!'" Tony T chuckled.

* * *

"Man, you niggas is mad wild as hell!" Floyd laughed with is crew and Dante's team as they stood watching Tank and his boys running naked up the street after just being stripped at gunpoint and forced to leave the Quickie Mart. "This how y'all get down back in Miami?"

"I'm feeling that shit!" Kaos stated while still laughing.

Dante smirked as he sat in the passenger seat of the Escalade watching the show. He shook his head and then looked at James. "J! Go ahead inside the store with Floyd and make the owner an offer. Let him know we'll pay him $5,000 a week for the use of his store, and we're also offering protection as well as help with whatever work he may need help with."

"I got you," James replied as he waved for Floyd to follow him.

"I really see why muthafuckas are all fucked up about this nigga!" Beast stated with a smile to Dante. "This nigga is really on some boss shit!"

THREE

Fish Man listened to what the muthafucka was telling him over the phone about what had happened to him and his whole team over on the east side of Brooklyn by some niggas with the young punk Floyd. Fish Man not only balled up his face in anger because he was being disrespected, but also because the niggas in New York claimed to be from Miami and supposedly friends of his.

"What was that about?" Gator asked Fish Man as his boy hung up the phone once he was finished talking with Tank.

Fish Man shook his while sitting behind his desk at his six-bedroom, five-bath estate that he and his lady, Shawna, lived in together. "Some clowns that claim to be from Miami just took back the Quickie Mart spot out in East Brooklyn."

"What's up with Tank and them niggas?" Gator asked. "They at war with these fools or what?"

Fish Man shook his head and replied, "From what this fool Tank says, he and the team we put out there with him got stripped naked and made to run up the street."

Gator burst out laughing after what Fish Man had just told him. "You mean some niggas ran down on Tank and his boys and clowned them niggas in the middle of the streets?"

"That's what he told me."

"Man, if them niggas let some clowns run down on them and bitch their ass up like that, then that's good for their ass! Where's their ass now?"

"Tank's at his lady's crib now. He says he ain't sure where the other niggas are."

Gator shook his head and waved his hand as he turned and left Fish Man's office while talking under his breath.

* * *

Dante arrived back to the hotel a few hours later after getting a good look around the city and even speaking with a few hustlers that quickly recognized him at first sight. Dante gave out a few business offers and got back some agreements as well, and a few other hustlers said they wanted to think about his offers, which was alright with Dante. He said he'd give them a few days to get back at him with an answer.

Once he was back at the suite, Dante unlocked and opened the door, just as his cell phone went off. He pulled it out and saw Alinna had called.

"What's up, shorty?"

"Dante, you out?" Vanessa asked him once she heard his voice.

"Naw! I'm at the suite," he answered Vanessa. "Where's Alinna at?"

"She's taking care of something, but we're on our way back to the suite now," Vanessa told him. "Alinna wants you out front when we pull up."

"Everything alright?"

"Yeah, boy. Just be out front in fifteen minutes."

Dante heard the call end after Vanessa hung up the phone. He was just sitting on the sofa when the suite door opened and in walked Rose, Emmy, Natalie, and the kids.

"Daddy!" Mya cried out happily after seeing her father. She then took off and rushed over to his side and jumped into his lap.

Natalie smiled at the sight of her husband and handed Damian over to Emmy. She then followed Dante Jr. and Andre Jr. over to the sofa on which Dante was sitting.

"Where y'all just coming from?" Dante asked his wife,

after receiving a kiss from her.

"Daddy, we went to go shopping, and then Natalie took us all to eat," Mya answered for Natalie.

"That's why you smell like pizza breath, huh?" Dante asked his daughter playfully before turning around and looking toward his son and nephew. "What's up, fellas? Y'all was taking care of Mya and Natalie, right?"

"We got this, Dad!" Dante Jr. told his father, earning a smile from Dante.

"Daddy, can we watch TV?" Mya asked her father while already climbing from his lap.

A second later, she took off to the back of the suite with both her brother and cousin behind her. Dante shook his head and smiled as he looked over at Natalie. She leaned in against his side and laid her head against his chest while he laid his arm around her.

"Where's Gomez at?"

"He's with James, Dre, and the others guys," Natalie answered. "And, yes, he was with us, along with ten other security men, Dante!"

"That's my girl!" Dante replied, bending his head down

and kissing Natalie's lips, only to have her wrap her arms up around his neck and deepen their kiss, before being interrupted by his ringing cell phone once again.

After pulling out of the kiss and receiving a protesting moan from Natalie, Dante dug out his cell phone and saw that Alinna was calling.

"Yeah, Alinna!"

"This is me, my husband!" Yasmine told Dante. "Can you come downstairs to the front of the hotel? We are pulling up to the hotel now, and Alinna wishes to show you something she has for you."

"I'm coming down now, Yasmine," Dante told her as he hung up the phone, only to have Natalie ask him what was going on.

"Alinna and the girls want me to come downstairs to see something Alinna bought for me," Dante explained to Natalie as he held out his hand. "Come with me."

Natalie smiled as she took his hand, stood up from the sofa, and allowed her husband to have his way, leading her to the front door of the suite.

* * *

Dante and Natalie stepped off the elevator a few minutes later and walked hand in hand through the hotel lobby to the exit. When they stepped outside, they saw a crowd of suit-wearing Japanese security men blocking off the front area of the hotel parking lot.

"Baby, there's Vanessa and the girls there!" Natalie told Dante, pointing to where Vanessa stood talking with the other Blackwell family women.

Dante released Natalie's hand as they headed over to the other girls, because Vanessa reached for him, only to cover his eyes.

"Vanessa, what the hell is going on?"

"Just relax and wait, boy!" Vanessa told him with a smile.

"Vanessa, you've got two—!"

"Boy, be quiet!" she told her brother, just as Alinna was turning into the hotel parking lot followed by a team of security filling the inside of an Escalade truck.

Vanessa waited a few moments until Alinna parked the new gift for Dante, and then she removed her hands from over his eyes.

"Now you can look, boy!"

Dante blinked his eyes a few times and then focused on the sight before him. He slowly began to smile his famous smirk while staring at Alinna, who was climbing from the driver's seat of a midnight-sapphire-colored new model Mercedes-Benz G63.

"What do you think?" Alinna asked as she walked over to her husband. "Is this a good enough replacement for the Audi I gave to Kyree?"

Dante chuckled lightly as he walked over to the G-Wagen. He looked inside at the dark bourbon leather seats. He then looked around the inside of the truck.

"I'm loving it, shorty! You did this?"

"Actually," Alinna started as she walked up beside Dante, "Yasmine picked this out for you. This was her gift for you since your birthday is this Friday. You'll get my gift soon as well as Natalie's gift."

He smirked as he shifted his eyes and looked over at Yasmine as she stood smiling and watching him. Dante motioned her over.

"Yes, my husband?" Yasmine said as she walked up to Dante.

"Thank you!" Dante told her, kissing her lips.

Afterward, he motioned for Natalie and then asked, "How about we go for a ride and then go over to my mother's house for dinner?"

"That sounds good," Alinna stated, getting agreeing nods from both Natalie and Yasmine.

* * *

Fish Man stepped off the elevator and headed up the hallway until he reached Diamond and Meline's hotel room. He then knocked on the door and waited a few moments. He was just about to knock again, when the door was unlocked and slowly opened up a little.

"What do you want, Kyle?" Diamond asked in her normal attitude she kept just for him.

"Diamond, come on, baby! Let me in!" Fish Man begged as he stepped forward, only for Diamond to stop him with her hand.

"Why are you here, Kyle?" Diamond asked him. "Why aren't you with that bitch Shawna? That's who you wanted, right?"

"Diamond, come on, baby!" Fish Man stated as he gently

grabbed her hand and held it up to his lips, kissing it while staring into her eyes.

He took another step forward and kissed Diamond while stepping into the hotel and getting past her this time. Unbeknownst to Fish Man, but not to Diamond who spotted him, Gage shook his head sadly after she closed the hotel room door behind her and Fish Man. Gage shut the hotel room door that was directly across from Diamond's room, and pulled out his phone and called to let Dante know that Fish Man was with Diamond.

* * *

Dante pulled up in front of his mother's house at 8:35 p.m. He parked the new G-Wagen and climbed out as Alinna, Yasmine, and Natalie all exited the Benz as well. He glanced right and then left and quickly spotted the Escalade with James, Gomez, and six backup security team members parked across the street.

Dante walked around the SUV with Natalie holding onto his arm, after she climbed out from the Mercedes on his side.

"I was wondering if you all was still coming!" Brenda stated, after opening her front door and seeing her son and three wives get out of the Benz.

"It's my fault we're late, Momma Blackwell," Alinna admitted as she held up the plastic bag with ice cream that she made Dante stop for. "We got a taste for ice cream!"

"She's got a taste, Momma!" Dante said, causing his mother, Yasmine, and Natalie all to burst out laughing while Alinna playfully rolled her eyes at him.

Once they were inside the house they could smell fried chicken. All three women sat down in the front room while Dante headed straight for the kitchen. Brenda smiled and shook her head watching her son, but then sat down across from the wives.

"We're waiting on Dwayne to get back. I sent him to the store to pick up some sodas," Brenda explained.

"Why didn't you just tell me to bring some, Momma?" Dante asked, walking back into the front room eating a piece of chicken.

"It's fine, sweetheart," Brenda told him as he sat down beside her. "So, how are things going so far?"

"You mean business or personal, Momma?" Dante asked, finishing his chicken wing.

"Both!" Brenda asked as her son left the room again.

She looked over to Alinna as her son's first wife spoke up.

"We've decided to stay here longer than planned, Momma Blackwell. Dante and the family have all decided to expand the Blackwell business out this way and in New Jersey as well," Alinna explained.

"We also want you to be a part of it, Momma," Dante stated as he entered the room drinking a glass of milk and sitting back beside his mother.

"What do you mean, Dante?" Brenda asked, looking from her son to his wife and then back to Dante.

"Momma Blackwell," Alinna started, getting Brenda's attention, "I've spoken with Dante, and he's told me of your past history as you've told it to him. And with how fast Dante moves, it would be great to have a second person to help with decisions, since the family would rather leave the major decisions to Dante and me."

"So, what do you say, Momma?" Dante asked as he lay against her shoulder. "Will you join your son and daughters-in-law?"

Brenda smiled down at her extremely handsome son. She

then ran her hand over his wavy hair and sighed. "Okay. I'll be there when you all need my help."

"Thanks, Momma!" Dante said, kissing his mother's cheek just as his phone went off. "Yeah, what's up, J?"

Dante listened to what James had to say, and then hung up. "Dwayne's outside. And Melody and this boyfriend she got just pulled up as well."

"Dante, behave!" Brenda told her son, seeing the look on his face.

Brenda stood up and went over to the front door. She unlocked it and swung it open, just as Dwayne stood in front of it.

"Perfect timing!" Dwayne told his wife, kissing her cheek before stepping inside the house.

"Momma, is Dante here?" Melody asked as she and her boyfriend, Norise, stepped up to the front door.

"He's inside," Brenda told her daughter with a smile as she allowed her daughter and Norise to enter the house.

FOUR

After Dante finished dinner, he took meals across the street to James and the others keeping watch in the Escalade at his mother's orders. On the way back to the house, his cell phone went off. He pulled it out and recognized the name but not the phone number. "What's up, Lieutenant?" he answered the call.

"How are you, Dante?" she asked. "I have the information you're looking for on those two people you asked me about."

"Where are you?" Dante asked while motioning over James and the others.

Dante listened to Lewis as she gave up her location. Dante stepped up to the front passenger window of the Escalade with Gomez inside. Dante then told the lieutenant to hold on while he gave James and Gomez directions of where to meet the lieutenant. He followed up by giving them instructions of what he wanted done.

"Lieutenant!" Dante called into the phone, after James pulled off.

"I'm here, Dante!"

"I have someone coming over to you now. Look for either a white guy with short black hair or a huge muscular guy."

"I'll contact you once I've spoken with your people."

After hanging up with Lieutenant Lewis, Dante slid his phone back into his pocket.

"What is it you want?" Dante asked.

"How?" Norise started, staring at Dante as the kingpin legend turned around to face him. "How'd you know I was standing here?"

"I heard the front door when it opened, and I saw your reflection in the window of the truck," Dante admitted, before asking again, "What do you want?"

"Ummmm," Norise started up before he took a deep breath and then continued, "look, Dante, I know we don't know each other, and even though the world may know who Dante Blackwell is, I don't know you really. Melody tells me you're a businessman, and I'm in the business of dealing with weed. But the dude I'm dealing with ain't really a major hustler, and I'm trying to really get in some major moves. So what I'm saying is that I got $48,000, and I'm trying to get on with you, my nigga. I know you work with some of everything, but weed is my thing."

"My sister sent you out here, huh?" Dante asked him as he walked over to stand beside his sister's boyfriend.

"Yeah!" Norise answered truthfully. "We spoke about it, and Melody told me if I came at you like a man, you would consider my offer. So here I am!"

Dante slowly nodded his head while pulling out his Black & Milds. He took out one of the cigars and remained quiet until the Black was lit and he was blowing smoke from his lips.

"Tell me something, boyfriend. Can you handle twenty-five pounds?"

Norise was surprised at first with the number Dante had thrown at him.

"Yeah. I can handle it!" he responded after he got control of himself.

"Alright," Dante said, nodding his head as he blew smoke from his mouth. "I'll have someone contact you in two days, but keep your money. Matter of fact, spend it on my sister. You work for me now. I'll have you a spot set up soon. Be ready to work!"

Dante left his sister's boyfriend standing out in front of his mother's house with a big smile on his face. Dante then spotted his sister peeking out the front window and staring straight at him. He walked up to the front door, only for Melody to meet him as she quickly swung it open.

"Dante, did you—?"

"Relax, baby girl!" Dante told Melody, cutting her off. "I put him on!"

Melody smiled after hearing what her big brother had just told her. She threw her arms around his neck and hugged him tightly. "Thank you, Dante!"

* * *

Dante relaxed with his mother as the two of them sat together on the couch. Alinna, Yasmine, and Natalie were sitting on the sofa while Dwayne was in his La-Z-Boy watching Will Smith's movie *I Am Legend*, which Melody and Norise brought with them to watch. Dante sat up from leaning down on his mother with his head on her chest as she rubbed his head. He then dug out his ringing phone to see Gomez was calling him.

"What's up, Gomez?" Dante answered the phone.

Dante sat listening a few minutes as Gomez explained to him what was going on. After finding out the location where his team was located, he then hung up the phone.

"My husband," Yasmine called out, watching Dante and seeing the change in his facial expression. "What is wrong?"

Dante simply nodded his head to her question and winked his eye at her. He then looked at his mother.

"Momma, how about we go for a ride? I got something to show you," Dante asked her.

"Dante, what are you—?"

"Momma Blackwell," Natalie spoke up, cutting off Brenda, "I mean no disrespect, but it's best to just follow Dante and not question him when he's like this."

Brenda looked over at Natalie and then back to her son, and she saw the expression on his face.

"Don't look like that. I'll go with you," Brenda said as she gently brushed her hand down Dante's face.

* * *

Dante left his mother's house and found the address Gomez had given to him over the phone, along with help from his mother. He pulled the G-Wagen through the front gate of a nice-sized house. He drove up the driveway and turned off into the front parking area beside the Escalade and instantly spotted two of his men posted at the door.

Dante climbed out of the SUV and then opened up the

passenger-side door for his mother as Alinna, Yasmine, and Natalie climbed from the back of the Benz. Dante then closed his mother's door and escorted her up to the front door.

"Dante, whose house is this?" Brenda asked her son as she followed Dante inside.

"You'll see," Dante replied, seeing James standing in the opening that led into the den.

"What's up, bruh?" James said before he nodded over toward the couch. "There goes your boy right there."

Dante shifted his attention over to the sofa and saw Gomez standing over a dark-skinned man and an older, redboned woman. Dante called to his mother, but when he looked over at her, he saw she was already staring at both the man and woman seated on the sofa.

"That's the nigga right there you wanted?"

"Brenda!" Antonio Mitchell said in disbelief, staring at his one-time girlfriend. "What are you doing here? What's going on?"

Brenda walked over to stand in front of Antonio and the woman who she recognized as her best friend at one time. "I bet you didn't think I would find you, did you, Abigail? My so-called friend all along wanted not only my sorry-ass man, but my life, huh?" Brenda addressed the woman.

"Brenda, it wasn't—!"

"Shut the hell up!" Brenda told her ex-best friend, her voice raising enough to cut off the other woman. She then looked back toward Antonio Mitchell and met his eyes. "Do you remember what I told you all those years ago, Antonio? I told you you would pay for what you did to me! Well now it's judgment day!"

"So, calling the devil himself is your way to get back at me, huh?" Antonio Mitchell asked, smirking as he cut his eyes over toward Dante. "Dante Blackwell. So you're doing Brenda's work now, huh? I wouldn't believe someone like you would do dirty work for someone like this!"

"Like what?" Dante questioned, and was up on Antonio Mitchell before homeboy could finish what he was saying. He had Antonio Mitchell up against his right eye socket. "Finish what the fuck you was saying, or has your punk ass had a change of heart?"

"Dante!" Brenda said in a calm voice, watching her son shove Antonio back into his seat and step back to stand beside her.

Brenda then walked back over to Antonio and said, "I

apologize, Antonio. Allow me to introduce my son, Dante Blackwell Jr. My first boyfriend I left and ended up with you!"

"Your son!" Antonio repeated, looking at Dante as the young killa stood staring at him with gun in hand.

"How you want this done, Momma?" Dante asked while still staring at Antonio. "Fast or slow?"

"Make it slow, sweetheart!" Brenda answered her son with a grin, only to hear Dante call out to his wife, Yasmine.

* * *

Brenda quietly sat back in the front passenger seat of her son's Mercedes after just watching Dante's third wife skillfully torture both Antonio Mitchell and Abigail Harris, until they both stopped breathing. Brenda looked over at the expression of her son while he quietly drove home. "What's on your mind, sweety?"

Dante lost his train of thought and looked over at his mother. "I'm good, Momma. I'm just thinking," he answered.

"About?"

"You remember when I was talking to you about this fool from back in Miami that moved out this way in New Jersey?"

"Fish Man! I remember!"

"I'm just thinking how it's possible to run a business and

deal with this beef at the same time, Momma."

"Dante, listen to me, sweetheart," Brenda told her son in a motherly tone. "I've spoken with your wife Alinna, and from everything she's told me about everything the two of you have gone through, you've changed from the Dante you once was. You've joined in on the business full time instead of part time, Dante. My advice to you is to go back to the Dante you used to be and let Alinna do what she does best: running the business part of the family. But assist her when she needs it. I'll do as much as I can, but do what you're known for. Do you understand me?"

Dante slowly nodded his head after listening to his mother's words. He then looked back at Alinna through the rear-view mirror, met his wife's eyes, and winked at her.

"I understand, Momma. I got you," Dante said.

FIVE

Alinna heard her son yelling out for her. She opened her eyes when the bedroom door flew open and Dante Jr. burst into the bedroom and jumped into the bed. Alinna rolled over to smile at her handsome son, just as he began pulling at her arm for her to get up.

"Dante Jr., what's wrong?" Alinna asked, sitting up on the bed.

"Dad wants you out front," Dante Jr. told his mother. "He's about to leave, and he wants to talk to you."

"Tell your father I'm coming," Alinna told her little man, smiling as he took off out of the bedroom.

She climbed out of bed and first headed to the bathroom and took care of her woman's needs. Five minutes later she was dressed in jeans and one of Dante's T-shirts.

Alinna left the bedroom and walked out to the front room where she heard voices, only first to see Gage leaning against the wall near the front door with his arms folded across his chest. She paused when she noticed the immediate family standing or sitting around the front room of the suite.

"What's going on in here? Everything alright?"

"Everything's cool, shorty," Dante spoke up from across the room while leaning against the dresser that held a television on top of it. "I wanna talk to everybody before me and the rest of the fellas leave."

"Where are you going?" Alinna asked as she sat down beside Vanessa.

Dante ignored Alinna's question and instead said, "I'ma make this quick because we got work to do. From now on, things are going back to how they was back before we got to where we are now. My mom made a good point yesterday. So as before, the women will have majority say when it comes to the business part of this family. Alinna will be at the head, and the guys will make sure there are no problems or issues with nobody, because we all know how things will turn out. Does anybody have anything to say?"

"Will things stay how they are concerning Fat . . . I mean Fish Man?" Harmony asked, causing a few of the family members to laugh.

"Nothing's changed with that!" Dante answered. "I'll

handle Fish Man and will keep everybody on point with that, but Kyree will still report to Alinna since it was a direct order from her to him. Are there any more questions?"

"Yeah!" Vanessa spoke up, drawing Dante's attention. "What happened to the suits, pretty boy? You back to the jeans and Air Max?"

"I'm back to the Dante you first met, baby Sis!" Dante told Vanessa, winking his eye at her.

Just then there was a knock at the suite door. Dante looked over at Gage and nodded. He watched his personal bodyguard unlock and open the door, and he saw his mother standing there. Dante smiled at the sight of her. He kissed her on the cheek when she walked over and stood beside him.

"Hey, Momma!"

"Hello, sweetheart," Brenda replied as she straightened out her gray pantsuit.

"Alright, family," Dante said, getting the family's attention. "From now on, Alinna and my mother will be the heads of the business. Alinna runs it, and my mother will assist her through everything. And, Yasmine?"

"Yes, my husband?" she replied.

"I need you to contact your father and have him send my mother his best bodyguard. Tell him I will pay the price for him or her if needed," Dante told his wife, receiving a bow from her in return.

Dante kissed his mother's cheeks and then first kissed Alinna, then Natalie, and finally Yasmine, before saying his goodbyes to everyone. He then started for the door with his brother behind him.

"James!" Alinna called out.

"Yeah, what's up, Alinna?" James looked back and answered, after hearing her call out his name.

"Watch my man's back, James," Alinna told him, in a tone that caused James to smile and nod his head in response before turning and following the guys out of the suite.

* * *

"Yo, Floyd!" Eddie said, tapping Floyd's arm and getting his attention away from texting on his cell phone.

"Yeah," Floyd answered, looking up and over at Eddie, only to see the boy nod out of the driver's window.

"Here comes Dante and them!" Eddie said, watching as Dante and his boys exited the hotel, and noticing how people stared at the five men.

Floyd climbed out of his Jeep Grand Cherokee SRT. He called out to Dante by waving at him to get his attention.

"What's good, Cuzo?" Dante asked, dapping up with Floyd. He then nodded to Eddie on the other side of the Jeep, before looking back at his cousin. "Where's your team at?"

"Waiting for us at Brooklyn Park now," Floyd answered, but then asked, "What's up? What happened to the suits?"

"Hung up in the closet. Let's go!" Dante told his cousin, walking off and heading over to his G-Wagen.

Dante followed the Jeep out of the hotel parking lot a few moments later and headed toward Brooklyn Park, where the rest of Floyd's team was waiting. Dante drove quietly and smoked one of his Black & Milds while he put together a plan inside his head. Dante saw Beast and the rest of Floyd's team by the time Gage pulled up to the area. Dante told Gage to keep the Benz running and to let down his window. He let out a loud whistle to get Floyd's attention and waved him over.

"What's good, Cuz?" Floyd asked as he walked up to Dante's window.

"Listen! We're gonna do this like this, Cuzo. Send me the

twins, and I'ma send my brothers, Dre and Tony, with you. We starting with Brooklyn, and then the rest of the boroughs. We're taking New York first and building here, but Jersey is our destination. I'm telling you this because we're moving fast out here. My advice is to let my brothers take leads and be ready to let your hammers sound off, because if shit gets stupid, it's probably gonna be Dre and Tony acting out!"

Dante nodded to both Dre and Tony T and then looked back at his cousin. "Text me the locations of the spots that are pulling in some cash, and we'll start from there!" Dante told Floyd.

Dante then waited as twins Kaos and Corrupt took Dre and Tony T's spots inside the G-Wagen. Dante began explaining to the twins exactly what was about to begin happening, finishing what he had to say by asking if they were ready to put in some work.

"We was wondering exactly when we was actually going to get in some play time!" Corrupt told Dante.

"Put us in, coach!" Kaos chimed in.

Dante nodded his head in approval of what he was hearing. He was definitely going to see what his younger soldiers were all about very soon.

* * *

Alinna left the hotel and first met up with a real estate agent and looked at a few new places for the family as well as Brenda and her husband. She and her mother-in-law then discussed different business ideas. Alinna even caught Brenda's idea after mentioning how the setup was that she and Dante had back in Phoenix with the Council Covenant.

"So basically what you're saying is that you want to build our own council?" Brenda asked Alinna while thinking on the idea a bit more.

"Dante wants the women to run the family business. So with me, you, Vanessa, and the rest of the women in the family as the council members, we can then make this work! Dante will have his say as always, but it will be us who control the council."

Brenda slowly nodded her head, looked back at Alinna, and said, "I like this idea. Let's do it!"

"First we need a building where we can set up the council," Alinna told her mother-in-law.

"I know the perfect place, my daughter," Brenda replied.

* * *

Boom! Boom! Boom!

Dante barely watched the hustler's body hit the ground after peeling back his top and putting three rounds to his face in front of his crew. Dante then shifted his eyes around to the other six dudes who stood staring at him like he was insane.

"Now! Do we understand each other, or is there somebody else here who doesn't agree with me taking over this area?"

Dante received no response, but he saw the facial expressions from the crew members.

"It's good to see we can come to an agreement. Look for somebody of my family to come by here to drop off your new product. But know that if I hear or suspect any disrespect, I will come back and kill each of you and your families. On the other hand, if you respect me and work hard, I will guarantee that each of you will have everything you want. More money than your kids' kids can spend. Remember what I said, because I will not repeat it!"

Dante then turned and walked away with James, Gage, and the twins following behind. But he kept his eye on the crew whose lieutenant he just laid out on the sidewalk—and whose last thoughts ran out all over the concrete and into the cracks of the sidewalk.

Once they were all inside the G-Wagen, Dante started the engine, and they pulled off to yet another trap spot that Lloyd had texted to him. Dante pulled out his phone just as Kaos called to him from the backseat.

"Yeah!"

"Big homie, you do know whose spot that used to be, right?" Kaos asked, leaning forward between the two front seats.

"I'm aware, youngin'," Dante answered. "But it don't even matter, since this nigga Gator fucks with this chump-ass clown Fish Man. The way I see it, them niggas are breathing their last breath once I run down on their ass!"

"That nigga Gator better breathe deep then!" Corrupt stated, smiling as he shook his head.

Dante caught Corrupt's comment and showed Gage the next location they were heading to just as his phone began ringing and cleared the screen with the trap house list.

"What's up, shorty?" Dante answered, after seeing Alinna was calling.

"Dante, where are you?"

"Everything alright?"

"Yes, Dante. I just need you to come and see something. Can you come by?"

"Send me the location and I'ma come through in a little while."

"Thank you."

After hanging up with Alinna, Dante looked over at Gage and said, "Change of plans. We're gonna see what's up with Alinna."

"What's up, D?" James spoke up, after hearing Alinna's name. "Alinna in trouble, fam?"

"Naw!" Dante answered, smirking back at his brother after hearing the concern in his voice. "She just wants me to see something. We about to roll real quick and see what's up."

* * *

"What's up?" Fish Man answered his ringing phone while still laid up with Diamond from spending the night with her.

"What the fuck's going on?" Gator yelled, once he heard Fish Man's voice over the line. "Where the fuck you at nigga?"

"I'm chilling right now. Why? What's up?"

"Fuck you mean?" Gator yelled. "Nigga, if you was out here handling business, you'd know what the fuck was going on!"

"How about calming the fuck down and telling me what the fuck you talking about, nigga!" Fish Man told his partner as he sat up in bed next to Diamond, who was still asleep.

"Muthafucka, we're losing spots out here in New York," Gator yelled again. "I just received another call after five other muthafuckas called in telling me some bullshit about this nigga Dante Blackwell showed up!"

"What the fuck did you say?" Fish Man yelled as he leapt out of the bed. "Who the fuck you just say, nigga?"

"You heard what the fuck I just said, muthafucka!" Gator told Fish Man. "Supposedly, that punk-ass nigga you was telling me about and who be on the news here in New York is fucking with my money, and you're missing in action all of a sudden!"

"Fuck all that shit you talking about? You at the crib?" Fish Man asked as he began picking up his clothes.

"I'ma meet you at your spot!"

Once he heard Gator hang up, Fish Man continued

dressing.

"So, you leaving now, huh?" Diamond called over to Fish Man.

"I gotta handle something!" he told her as he grabbed up his things.

"Well, you coming back, right?" Diamond asked him, seeing him toss some money on top of the night table.

"I'ma call you later," Fish Man called out as he rushed out of the hotel room, leaving Diamond on the bed but missing the smile that was on her face.

* * *

Dante excused himself from the conversation going on among him, Alinna, his mother, and the leasing agent overseeing the sale of the office building that his wife and mother wanted. He then pulled out his ringing phone he gave to Diamond and Meline.

"Yeah! What's going on, Diamond?" he answered, glancing back over where Alinna and the others stood continuing their conversation.

"Boo, I don't know what the hell you're doing out there, but you got Kyle and his friend Gator losing their minds!"

"What's going on, Diamond? Where you at?"

"I'm still in the room."

"So what's going on?"

Dante listened to Diamond as she told him about the last few minutes since Fish Man got a call from his partner and she saw the panicked look on his face before he rushed from the room half-dressed. Dante stood smirking and nodding his head in agreement at what Diamond had just reported to him.

"Where's Meline at?"

"She's probably in the other room. You wanna talk to her?"

"Just tell Meline to call me later."

After hanging up the phone, Dante called up Dre.

"What's up, fam?"

"Be on point, fam! I just got a call from Diamond, and this clown Fish Man and his boy Gator just found out we're here."

"About time!"

"Keep handling business, Dre. We wait until we get out to Jersey to show out!"

"I got you, fam. I'ma let Tony T and them know what's the deal."

Dante hung up with Dre and started back over toward

Alinna and the others, when his phone went off again. He dug it out and smirked when he saw who was calling.

"Blood clot!" Wesley sung into the phone happily. "What go on, me brethren?"

"You guys here?" Dante asked.

"Yes, sir!" Wesley answered.

"I'm on my way!" Dante told his brother, before hanging up the phone and walking over to Alinna and whispering in her ear. He let her know he had to handle something but he'd call her in a little while.

"What do you think about the building?" Alinna asked Dante as he kissed his mother's cheek.

"I like it. Get it!" Dante told her, motioning James and his team to follow him as he headed for the exit.

SIX

Alinna got back to the hotel after finishing up with the leasing agent and buying the eleven-story building near their new mega-mansion that the family was going to move into in Buffalo. While she was sharing pictures of the new mansion with Natalie and the rest of the women, her mouth dropped open when she saw her sister walk into the suite.

"Amber!" Vanessa cried in shock when she saw her sister walk in with Wesley following her.

Vanessa then leapt off the sofa at the same time as Harmony, Alinna, Keisha, and Maxine all followed.

"What are you doing here?" Alinna asked Amber with a big smile, after releasing her sister.

Vanessa got in line next to hug Amber.

"Dante sent for us," Amber told Alinna as she hugged the other women. "Dante wanted his brother out here to play with him. From what I hear, Dante's back to his hell-raising ways and he needs his brothers to back his ass up!"

"That's what it seems like!" Harmony said playfully while

rolling her eyes at Dante, who stood talking with Wesley and Gage.

Dante then winked over at Kaos and Corrupt.

Once the women got Amber back inside their crowd, they found out that Dominic and Carmen Saldana were taking care of things back in Phoenix. Dante then interrupted their time just as there was knocking at the suite door and Gage walked over to answer it.

"What the fuck!" Tony T yelled as soon as he saw Wesley enter the suite.

"What go on, brethren?" Wesley said with a smile as he embraced Tony T and then Dre.

Wesley then looked at the young boy and the big guy who was a little smaller than Dre and was standing next to a cute brown-skinned younger female.

"Who dem, Rastaman?" he asked as he nodded toward Beast and Nina.

After Dante made introductions, he then brought everybody up to date on what was told to him about Fish Man and Gator knowing he was now in New York.

"I'll see what Kyree has to say when he calls me tomorrow,

since it's Friday," Alinna told Dante. "Also, we can move into the new house by tomorrow afternoon. Everything was taken care of by a lawyer Momma Blackwell introduced me to."

"That's right on time!" Dante replied, but then asked, "What about my momma's place, Alinna?"

"She's agreed to stay at one of the detached houses off the main house," Alinna announced to him.

"Wait a minute!" Amber said, getting everyone's attention. "You say one of the detached houses from the main house? Just how big is this house actually?"

"Let's just say it's bigger than both the mansions in Miami and out in Phoenix," Vanessa told Amber.

"Boy, do you ever stop?" Amber said to Dante as she looked over at him and shook her head.

"After New York and New Jersey, then you can ask me that question again!" Dante told Amber with a smirk. "We got two more family members on the way out here. Both Monica and Nash are getting transferred out here for some time until things are under control, and then they're flying back out to Phoenix."

"So what do we all control now, Dante?" Alinna asked her husband.

"Truthfully," Dante started, "half of Brooklyn!"

"This boy is just too damn much!" Vanessa said, smiling at Dante and then shaking her head.

Dante winked at Vanessa, which caused her to laugh, and then he looked over at Alinna. "I'ma give you and your girls a list of the new spots we now control, and some of them already have workers ready to get going. You have any problems just let me now and I'll deal with it, but they know what my promise was to them. I've already contacted Kevin Kim and should be getting a shipment out here by tomorrow night. So it's time to get to work. Yeah! There's also gonna be some weed on that shipment. It goes to my sister's boyfriend, so set that to the side for me," Dante said.

"Where are you going now?" Alinna asked as Dante and his brothers turned to leave.

"There's work to do. I'ma hit you later on, and Nina now works with you and your girls. Call me if you need me."

Alinna shook her head as her husband exited the suite followed by this brother. She then looked over at Brenda, only to see her husband's mother smiling proudly while staring at the front door.

* * *

Fish Man left Gator in the office after Shawna announced Kyree was at the house waiting on the back patio for him. Fish Man headed downstairs toward the back of the house to the patio where Shawna and a few of her friends were. They were doing the same bullshit they were always doing.

"Yo, Kyree!" he called out, seeing Kyree talking with one of Shawna's homegirls that he didn't like too much himself.

"Fish Man, what's up?" Kyree answered.

Kyree told Marsha, one of the girls who Shawna introduced him to, he would get back to her. He then walked over to Fish Man, who was waiting for him.

"My fault for getting here so late, but I just found a new spot out this way, and I had to handle a few things," Kyree explained.

"It's cool!" Fish Man told Kyree, motioning him into the house. "Guess who is here in New York?"

"Who that?" Kyree asked, even though he was sure he already knew, since he had been hearing Dante's name all over the city.

"Word is this nigga Dante Blackwell is out here in

Brooklyn," Fish Man told Kyree, glancing over to him as they started up the stairs.

"Fish, you serious?" Kyree asked him, playing the worried emotion. "You seen this nigga Dante out here for real?"

"Naw! I ain't seen 'im yet!" Fish Man admitted as he led Kyree into his office where Gator was waiting.

"What up, Gator, my nigga?" Kyree said, dapping up with homeboy.

"So, you finally decided to get with the winning team, huh?" Gator asked with a smile. "Well, did Fish Man tell you who else is in town out there in New York?"

"I was just telling him!" Fish Man told Gator, before he looked back at Kyree and said, "We ain't seen this nigga Dante out there. But the muthafuckas who work for us say there's some dude out there claiming to be Dante Blackwell, and he's been costing us some fucking money at different locations over there in Brooklyn!"

"So basically we're not sure it's Dante, right?" Kyree asked. "Fish Man, you and I both know how this nigga Dante gets down. If there ain't a pile of bodies out there in Brooklyn, and I mean a pile, then it ain't Dante. We both know how that fool can get down, and if they ain't say nothing about a huge muthafucka with this Dante, then it ain't Dante. Dre don't let Dante play alone! You see Dante, you gonna see Dre. Period!"

Fish Man heard the truth behind what Kyree had just said. He then relaxed a little more at hearing Dante Blackwell himself wasn't nearby. But he was still heated that he and Gator now had problems to deal with out in Brooklyn with whoever this supposed Dante Blackwell guy was causing trouble and fucking up cash flow.

* * *

Dante watched as both Monica and Nash Johnson walked out onto the lobby floor at the airport after just landing in New York. He locked eyes with her as she looked directly at him. She was unable to miss Dre's huge body along with Tony T, James, Gage, and Wesley—who was upset because he couldn't finish smoking his joint once they arrived inside the airport.

"Hey, you!" Monica said happily as James took her bags. She then wrapped her arms around Dante's neck and hugged him tightly. "I actually missed you, Dante!"

"I missed you too, Monica!" Dante replied while holding onto her small waist and then giving her a kiss. "Thanks for coming."

"Why wouldn't I? You said you needed me, so here I am!" Monica told Dante as she smiled and then released him.

"What's up, Nash?" Dante said, looking over at his gunman and Monica's backup help.

"What's up, boss man?" Nash said, smiling as he nodded to his boss and the guy he learned to respect in such a short time and considered a friend. "I got a favor to ask."

"Nash!" Monica cried, shooting her partner a look.

"What is it, Nash?" Dante asked, shaking his head and chuckling.

"I had a package sent out here. Can we pick it up at the post office?" Nash asked.

Dante shook his head and was still chuckling as he wrapped his arm around Monica's shoulders. He started toward the exit.

"Was that a yes or no?" Nash called out.

Once they were all outside and climbed into the G-Wagen, Dante had Dre sit up front while he, Monica, Tony T, and James got in the back. He told Gage they were going to the post office for Nash, and then he sat telling Monica and Nash about everything going on, as well as his future plans. Gage pulled the Benz into the post office parking lot while everyone sat waiting as Nash went inside.

"Dante!" Monica said, getting his attention. "How did everything go with meeting your mother when you got out here?"

"Everything went good," Dante answered. "You're about to meet her in a little while."

"Dante!" Dre called out. "Here comes your boy now."

Dante looked out the window to see Nash exiting the post office and carrying an extra-large black leather duffel bag with a handful of papers. Dante waited until James helped out with the bag, and then both guys got back inside the Benz.

"What's up with the bag, Nash?"

"Dis the same way the blood clot boy had dem gunz dem last time!" Wesley stated, staring at the duffel bag. "Where me AK, rude boy?"

"Good memory, Wesley," Nash told him. "I made sure there's at least one AK-47 inside for you."

"Blood clot!" Wesley sung happily.

"You brought guns, huh?" Dante asked with a smile.

"Small and big toys, boss man!" Nash told him. "I also

bought you a new vest since Monica told me you left your last one back in Phoenix."

"She told you, huh?" Dante stated, cutting his eyes over toward Monica, only to have her roll her eyes at him.

SEVEN

After the arrival of Monica and Nash, Dante set the two of them up inside his new field office with the New York DEA location. Dante and the rest of the family spent the remaining time through the week taking over the different boroughs around New York while the women of the family went about getting things taken care of with buying and setting up the new building the family bought for the Blackwell Council. They also moved the family from the hotel to their new thirteen-bedroom, eighteen-bath, eight-car garage mega-mansion, which all the women fell in love with instantly.

By Friday, which was Dante's twenty-second birthday, Alinna had set up a birthday party of which he knew nothing about but she was sure he would love. She had remembered that Fish Man visited the same night club every Friday night.

"Daddy!" Mya screamed as she burst into the master bedroom at the new mansion and caught Dante brushing his teeth. She ran right up beside him and threw her arms around his waist. "Happy birthday, Daddy!"

Dante rinsed out his mouth and then dried his face. He then tossed his towel onto the sink and turned to his daughter, picked her up, and kissed her cheek. "Thank you, baby girl. You remembered Daddy's birthday!"

Mya hugged her father's neck, kissed his cheek, and then loudly said, "You got to come with me, Daddy."

Dante lowered his daughter back to her feet and then allowed her to lead him by the hand from the master bedroom and out the door. Dante couldn't help the smile on his lips as Mya led him downstairs, bypassing the elevator, and headed to the bottom floor, where he could smell breakfast.

"About time you two showed up!" Alinna said, smiling at the sight of both her husband and Mya.

Alinna walked out of the kitchen, got up on her toes, and wrapped her arms around his neck to passionately kiss him.

"Was that my birthday present?" Dante asked as he held her around the waist, both hands gripping her ass once the kiss ended.

"No!" Alinna answered, smiling up at the holder of her heart. "That was because I love you! Come on!"

"Where we going?" Dante asked as he and Alinna made

their way over to the glass double doors that led out to the custom pool in the backyard.

"You'll see!" Alinna told him as she opened the patio door and led Dante onto the back patio.

"Happy birthday!"

Dante was caught off guard and slowly smiled. He saw the entire Blackwell family, Natalie's parents, Yasmine's father, business associates, and friends from back in Miami. Dante was then rushed by his kids and nephew. He hugged each of them and then began hugging his family and friends, starting with his mother and sister.

"Zoe Papi! Rafael!" Dante exclaimed, embracing both of them. "I'm surprised you two came out here and didn't just send word to me for my birthday."

"You no expect me to come see me brethren on his birthday?" Rafael asked, smiling at Dante.

"How could I miss the chance to catch up with the baddest muthafucka I know? Happy birthday, gangster!" Zoe Papi added.

Dante then hugged and talked with Dominic and Carmen, and then he walked over and spoke with his father-in-law,

Kevin Kim, who introduced Dante to a young-looking Japanese man named Jung. Kevin told Dante that Jung was his best bodyguard. Dante then called over his mother and introduced her to her new personal bodyguard.

* * *

Once breakfast was served and everyone sat down to eat, both Rose and Emmy directed their new staff. Alinna then pulled both Natalie and Yasmine off to the side.

"What's wrong, Alinna?" Yasmine asked, once the three of them were a short distance away from the others.

"Everything's fine, Yasmine. I just wanted to know if you both had Dante's gifts ready?" Alinna questioned them.

"I have Dante's gift ready," Yasmine answered with a smile.

"My gift for Dante arrived this morning. It's ready," Natalie told Alinna, also smiling.

Alinna nodded her head and then said a few more words to both women. She then returned to Dante's side and received a smile once he noticed her. She gave him a kiss just because.

After the food was gone and breakfast was finished, Alinna nodded to Yasmine and then stood to her feet and called for everyone's attention.

"First, I want to thank everyone for coming to my husband's party for his twenty-second birthday. If you give us a few minutes, Yasmine, Natalie, and I first would like to give Dante his gifts, and then you all can give him yours."

"Blood clot!" Wesley cried out. "Me don't know what to give me brethren when the Rastaman has everything already."

"I'm sure your gift will be good enough, Wesley," Alinna told him, smiling while everyone laughed.

Once everyone calmed down, Yasmine approached her husband and offered him an oak wood box that had his name printed across the front in gold letters.

"This is a special gift I had designed for you. I hope you love them, my husband."

Dante took the box from his wife and then surprised Yasmine by pulling her down into his lap. He first kissed her and then turned to focus on the box. As he opened it, he slowly smiled when he saw the twin chrome .40 calibers that were edged in gold. One of the guns had his full name engraved in gold, and the other had her name. There were also two extra chrome and gold magazines in between both pieces.

"Now this is what I'm talking about, baby!" Dante told Yasmine, smiling as he kissed her again, only longer and more passionately this time.

"Yasmine!" Natalie spoke up, interrupting the kiss between her husband and Yasmine. "Can I have him for a few minutes, please?"

Yasmine kissed Dante one more time before she got up from his lap. She then stepped back, smiling down at Dante as Natalie took his hand.

"Come with me, baby!" Natalie told Dante, pulling him up from his seat.

She led her husband around to the far right side of the mansion as all the guests followed. They walked around to the garage and stopped in front of the middle garage door. Natalie smiled back at Dante and then pressed the remote button, causing all eight garage doors to begin lifting.

"Wait right here!" Natalie told Dante as she walked into the garage.

Dante watched as his wife walked inside and stopped next to a metallic black and orange-edged car with which he wasn't familiar. He continued waiting and watching as Natalie got inside the car. After she started it up and it barely purred, she backed the car out. He instantly recognized the style of car it was.

"Blood clot!" Wesley cried out recognizing the car as he and the rest of the men crowded around Dante.

Natalie then parked the car in front of Dante and climbed back out with a huge smile on her face.

"So what do you think, baby?" Natalie questioned as she tossed Dante the keys to his new car.

Dante caught the keys out of the air and shook his head. He smiled as he walked over to the brand new model Bugatti Veyron. He then looked over at a smiling Natalie and motioned her over to him.

"You do know I love you, right?" Dante asked Natalie as he wrapped his arms around his wife.

"I know!" Natalie answered, smiling as she reached up and wrapped her arms around his neck. "I love you too, Dante, with everything in me. I do!"

* * *

Dante enjoyed the party and kicking it with his family and friends. He ended up carrying his daughter, Mya, around during the entire party since she refused to leave his side, even when she had to eat lunch. She sat in his lap and ate with him until Brenda had her go and eat with the other kids. He found himself soon holding his youngest boy, Damian, after Natalie brought him over to him. Dante then looked around for Alinna and found her inside the house talking on the phone with her face balled up in anger.

"Vanessa!" Dante called out to his sister, handing his son to his auntie. "I'm gonna be right back."

Dante left the back patio, entered the house, and walked up to Alinna as she was hanging up the phone.

"What is it?" Dante asked.

"This was supposed to be a quiet birthday, Dante!" Alinna told her husband with a sigh. "That was Kyree calling. He says Fish Man and his friend Gator sent two teams out to two of our new spots. They took control again, Dante!"

Dante chuckled and then kissed his wife as he walked back out on the patio and released a loud whistle to which his team instantly responded. "Let's get going! We've got work to do fellas!"

* * *

"Alinna, what's happened?" Natalie cried out as she and the other women rushed over to Alinna as she exited the house.

Alinna watched as the guys all followed Dante back into the house. She then turned back to face her girls and also her mother-in-law.

"Kyree just called me. He says Fish Man and Gator just took back two of our spots out in Brooklyn, so now Dante's going to deal with it!"

"Well!" Brenda spoke up, drawing the women's attention to her. "Since Dante and the men are dealing with this small issue, we have time to handle a few business plans of our own! Alinna, why don't you send two of the girls to make sure things at the new club you've bought for Dante and yourself are set up, and each of us can deal with other business matters we have been seeing to as well."

Alinna nodded her head in agreement as she got right to work assigning both Vanessa and Harmony to handle things at the new club. She then led the rest of the women back inside to get to work.

* * *

Dante broke the guys into two teams and got the locations

of the spots Fish Man and Gator had gone after from Alinna. Dante then climbed into the G-Wagen with James, Gage, Floyd, Beast, and Norise while Dre, Tony T, Wesley, and a team went with them.

Dante loaded the new .40 calibers that Yasmine bought for him as Gage was pushing the G-Wagen back across town into Brooklyn. Dante slammed the magazine into the .40 with Yasmine's name on it. After putting a round inside the chamber, he filled the open slot inside the magazine and then repeated the same with the other .40.

"What's the plan, Cuz?" Floyd asked from the backseat of the G-Wagen.

"The plan is to erase every face that's out there, because they're not with us!" Dante told his cousin as he was lighting up the joint Wesley gave him before leaving the mansion.

* * *

"Bomba clot!" Wesley yelled as he jumped from the back of Dre's new all-black 2009 Hummer H2 SUV, with his AK-47 in both hands. He began letting the AK speak just seconds before Tony T and the rest of the team in the Escalade began letting their bangers sing as well.

Dre pulled out his .45 and hopped from the Hummer after seeing two dudes duck off from in front of Brooklyn Park and hide behind a parked SUV a few feet from the Hummer.

"What's up, fella?" Dre yelled.

Boom! Boom! Boom!

Dre dumped on the two clowns that were hiding out, just as they looked up to see who he was. He then dumped two more rounds into each body, and then turned and jogged back over to the Hummer.

* * *

"This is your lucky day!" Dante told the muthafucka he was standing over, pointing his .40 down at his face. "I'ma let you live this one time, but I want you to go back and tell Fish Man's bitch ass that I'll be by to see him soon. Also, let Gator know that since he wants to be a part of this shit, he can expect a visit from me real soon too!"

Boom!

Dante blew a hole in homeboy's thigh and then turned and left him laid out and screaming at the top of his lungs in pain. Dante walked over to where the G-Wagen was waiting, with both James and Gage following behind. Once they got inside the Benz and ignored the bodies laid out in the streets, Dante pulled out his phone as Gage was driving off. He punched in the lieutenant's phone number.

"Lieutenant Lewis here!"

"This Dante. There's an issue out on—!"

"I've already heard, Dante," she cut him off. "Your wife Alinna called and warned me you were handling something, and I just heard the call on my radio. You're not still there, are you?"

"No!"

"Good! I'll take care of this and call you once I'm finished."

After hanging up with Lewis, Dante then called Alinna.

"Where are you?" Alinna asked, answering on the start of the second ring.

"On the way home," he replied. "Wait until tomorrow and let the team know they can get back to work."

"You spoke to Lewis?" Alinna inquired. "I told her to be ready for the call."

"She told me you called. But she's handling it now."

"Are you okay?"

"Yeah! I'll be home in a minute."

"Love you."

After hanging up with Alinna, Dante's phone began ringing again, and he saw it was Dre.

"Yeah!"

"Fam, this is Tony T. That's taken care of."

"Everybody good?"

"Everybody's good, fam."

"I'ma check y'all when y'all get back to the house."

Dante hung up with Tony T and then dropped the phone into his lap. His mind then raced to thoughts of getting at Fish Man and Gator.

EIGHT

Lieutenant Lewis heard all the stories, but she was unable to truly believe it until that very moment when she pulled up her Jaguar to the surrounding massacre. She saw at least six covered bodies laid out all over the street and parking lot. She found a place to park and then climbed from her car. Instantly, microphones and cameras were shoved into her face and questions were yelled at her.

Lewis ignored the reporters and walked off, crossing the yellow crime scene tape. She was approached by a uniformed officer and told that Detective Aaron Howard was overseeing the investigation. She thanked the officer and approached the detective from behind.

"What do we have, Detective?" Lieutenant Lewis asked, stopping beside the squatting detective as he was looking over a body.

The detective looked over and saw Lewis standing over him. Detective Howard dropped the sheet back over the body and then stood to his full five-foot-ten height.

"Looks like we have a small war zone out here. There's a total of eleven bodies and one wounded."

"One wounded?"

"Yeah. He's over with the EMT getting ready to head to the hospital. He took a bullet to the right thigh."

Lieutenant Lewis looked over at the EMT van and told the detective she would be back. She then made her way to the van. She motioned to the female paramedic and told her she wanted to speak with the wounded man, receiving the EMT's approval. Lewis climbed into the back of the van and sat down beside the young man.

"How do you feel?"

"How the fuck you think I feel?" he yelled, spitting out his words in anger. "I'm fucking shot, and who the hell is you?"

Lewis showed the young man her identification and shield, and then asked, "What's your name?"

"What the hell you wanna know my name for?"

"How am I supposed to talk to you if I don't know your name?" she asked him. "I'm not here to arrest you. I just want to find out what's happened out here. Who's responsible for all those bodies out there?"

"I don't know shit about nothing!" he told the lieutenant and then shut his eyes.

Lieutenant Lewis saw no more reason to speak with the young man, but she planned on keeping an eye on him. She thanked him and then climbed from the back of the EMT van. She then saw the detective on his phone arguing with someone, so she pulled out her cell phone and pulled up Dante's number as she walked to the side of the scene.

"Yeah!"

"Dante, it's Megan."

"What's up, Lieutenant?"

"I'm at the scene now and it's a mess out here. But I just met the responding detective who's overseeing the investigation, and truthfully he's a hot mess. I'm going to have to watch him closely. Also, you made a mistake and left one person alive."

"That wasn't a mistake!" Dante informed the lieutenant. "I left him with a message to report back to Fish Man and his boy Gator. But tell me something though. Is this detective you just mentioned gonna be a problem?"

"Possibly!"

"What's this detective's name?"

"Aaron Howard."

"I'll call you back."

After Dante hung up the phone, Lewis looked back where Detective Howard was standing, and saw that he was still arguing on his cell phone with someone. She then turned and walked back to her Jaguar.

* * *

Dante hung up on Lewis and then called his mother's number. He sat staring out the passenger window of the G-Wagen listening to his mother's number ringing.

"Hello!"

"Momma, it's Dante."

"Hey, sweety. How did everything go?"

"We are on our way home now," Dante informed her. "But I need you to do something though."

"What is it, Dante?"

"I need you to contact your friend and have him call me. I need to talk to him."

"I'll do that right now, sweetheart."

After ending his phone call with his mother and pulling up

Monica's new cell number, Dante waited two rings, when the phone was answered.

"Yeah, Dante?"

"I need some information."

"I'm not surprised. What's the name of this person?"

"Detective Aaron Howard."

"Detective, Dante?"

"I need all the information you can find on this guy. Call me back when you got it, Monica!"

"Whatever, boy."

After hearing Monica hang up, Dante called the lieutenant back.

"Lieutenant Lewis."

"It's Dante. I just contacted my friend with the DEA. They're looking into a few things for me, and I'm passing the information off to you to deal with this guy, unless you want me to deal with dude my way."

"I'll handle it, Dante."

"Good!" he replied, before hanging up the phone with the lieutenant.

* * *

Fish Man exited the hotel after visiting Diamond but catching Meline in the room by herself. He then walked out to Kyree's Audi with a smile on his face, with the thought of the past hour and a half he spent alone with Meline. He walked around to the passenger side and then climbed into the Audi.

"What's up, my nigga?" Kyree said once Fish Man was inside the car.

"What's up, player?" Fish Man replied. "Good looking out on coming to snatch me up."

"Where's ya ride at anyway?" Kyree asked, glancing over at Fish Man and seeing homeboy with his head laid back and his eyes closed shut.

Fish Man heard his phone begin to ring before he could answer Kyree. He dug out his phone and saw Gator was calling. "Yeah!"

"Where the fuck you at?"

Fish Man opened his eyes and lifted his head from the back of his headrest after hearing the tone of Gator's voice.

"I'm with Kyree," Fish Man answered. "What the fuck's wrong with you now?"

"Muthafucka! This shit is really starting to piss me the fuck off!" Gator yelled into the phone. "I just got a call from this nigga Spider. Whoever the fuck this muthafucka is who's supposed to be that Blackwell nigga, dude just took back not one but both spots we just took. And this muthafucka sent us a message!"

"What message?" Fish Man asked, sounding a little worried now.

"This muthafucka says he's coming to see us soon!" Gator told Fish Man. "Where the fuck you at? You coming out to the hospital to holla at Spider?"

"What hospital is he at?" Fish Man asked, shaking his head.

After hanging up the phone after getting the name of the hospital, Fish Man heard Kyree speak up. "What's up, Fish, my nigga?"

Fish Man repeated the same story to Kyree he was just told and then said, "We need to ride out over to Brooklyn General. I wanna talk to this nigga Spider."

* * *

Kyree pulled inside Brooklyn General ten minutes later and found an open place to park the Audi. After he shut off the engine, he and Fish Man climbed out of the car. They walked across the parking lot and entered the hospital. Kyree followed behind Fish Man to the elevator. But he noticed the expression on Fish Man's face after he heard the news about the takeover in Brooklyn and the Bronx and the way Dante's family strong-armed back and left behind a pile of bodies.

Once they got to the third floor where Spider's room was located, Kyree followed Fish Man off the elevator. Kyree pulled out his phone and sent a quick text while he continued to follow Fish Man.

"Here it is!" Fish Man announced as the two of them stopped in front of Spider's hospital room.

Both he and Kyree entered the room to find Gator standing beside the bed while the boy Spider sat up talking. But Spider paused when Fish Man and Kyree walked in.

"About time you decided to show up!" Gator stated, shooting Fish Man a look.

Fish Man ignored Gator as he walked up beside Spider's bed. He saw he was okay other than his thigh was wrapped up.

"How you feeling, lil' nigga?" Fish Man asked.

"Like shit!" Spider answered. "Fish Man, I'ma be real with you, my nigga. I don't know how the fuck you got this lunatic after you, but dude ain't playing, son! Dude says he's coming for you and your nigga Gator!"

"How'd you get away?" Kyree asked, even though he already knew.

"He wanted me to tell Fish Man and Gator that he was coming to see them real soon!" Spider answered Kyree.

"Tell me how this nigga looked you're talking about?" Fish Man asked Spider, feeling his heart speeding in his chest.

"Son, about five foot eleven or maybe six foot and got a slim but muscular build. Dude's got a six-pack of golds at the bottom of his mouth, and homeboy had these two boys with him who move just as deadly as he's moving. What's crazy is that one of his boys was a crazy-as-hell white boy who broke a nigga's neck in the middle of gun play, Fish Man! This shit's for real, my nigga!"

Fish Man recognized Dante's description and suddenly felt light-headed. He was out in the hallway before he realized it as he headed toward the elevator in a hurry.

NINE

Dante enjoyed the rest of his birthday that Friday with Alinna and the rest of the family. He gave them off that day; however, he and the rest of the guys in the family—both old and new members—went hard in the streets afterward, gaining control over New York. In fact, it was a lot easier than he expected. Although most hustlers wanted to fuck with him and his family based on his legendary past, most of them knew what the outcome would be if they refused to either buy their product from him or join his team. He still dealt with the hardheaded hustlers who wanted to test Dante's gangster mentality, but those individuals only ended up adding to the body count that the NYPD was continuing to collect.

After gaining control over New York and then moving into New Jersey, Dante had the family move around New Jersey a little differently than when dealing in New York. He wanted Fish Man and Gator to know that he was on their part of town now. He even heard from Kyree through Alinna one night that Fish Man was hiding out and letting Gator and Kyree run the business now.

Dante received a call from Diamond a few days after hearing about Fish Man. He got word from her that Fish Man was hiding out in Albany with Shawna, but that he still met with her and Meline on Fridays. Dante began putting together a plan and setting things up for the coming Friday. Dante then brought the news to the family, and both Alinna and Vanessa wanted to be there when everything was supposed to go down with Fish Man.

Plans changed when Gator brought pressure to the family by first going at one of the new spots out in Rochester and then hitting another spot in Manhattan. Dante had given those areas to Eddie to run, but he wound up with two bullets to the chest and one to the stomach.

When they arrived at Manhattan Hospital, they found out Eddie was laid up in a coma. Dante stood and dealt with his cousin Lisa, who was blaming him for what had happened to her boyfriend. He felt his anger boil over after hearing his cousin confess that she was pregnant with Eddie's baby.

"Dante!" Alinna yelled as he tore out of Eddie's hospital room. She took off after him, catching him just outside. "Baby, where are you going?"

"To end this shit!" Dante told her, before turning and walking off.

"Shit!" Alinna cried as she turned to rush back to the room, just as James and Gage shot past her following behind Dante.

Alinna shook her head and returned to the room, only to catch everyone's eyes as soon as she stepped inside.

"Alinna, where's Dante?" Brenda asked her daughter-in-law.

"He said he's going to end this, Momma Blackwell!" Alinna admitted.

"Hell naw!" Vanessa cried out as she dug out her cell phone. "I'm calling Andre."

* * *

Once Dante got outside the hospital and climbed into his G-Wagen, he pulled out his phone and called Kyree.

"What's up, Dante?"

"Text me Gator's address."

"Dante, I don't know it. But I do now where his girl lives at with her sister."

"Text me the address, now!" Dante said, before hanging

upon Kyree.

"We grabbing up this clown's people?" Gage asked while he glanced over at Dante.

"Naw!" Dante answered as his phone vibrated inside his hand. He looked at the text message and then held the phone out to Gage and said, "We gonna get this fool to come to us."

"Then he's dead!" James finished from the backseat.

Dante looked back at James through the rear-view mirror and gave him a small smile. "That's pretty much how it's gonna play out!" Dante explained.

* * *

Dante found the address Kyree had given him, only to pull up in front of a two-story house where he noticed a car pulling up and slowing beside his G-Wagen. Dante sat staring out the driver's window from the passenger window as the window on the Audi slid down.

"What's up, family?" Kyree asked, nodding over to Dante.

"What are you doing here?" Dante asked him, staring hard at Kyree and still feeling oddly about the boy.

"I figure I could help out with getting Gator's girl to let me inside, and then you three just kick in the door. This ain't

Brooklyn or New Jersey," Kyree explained to Dante. "Robin knows me, and she'll let me in."

Dante stared at Kyree a few moments and thought over what the young hustler just said. But he came up with his own idea instead and called back to James.

"Go with Kyree. Hit my cell phone once you're inside and you got both girls and whoever else is inside the house under control," Dante explained.

Dante still stared at Kyree as he and James climbed out from the G-Wagen. Dante then turned his head once James shut the back door, which broke his stare. "Gage, go ahead and drive around the block."

* * *

Less than five minutes later, waiting at the end of the block, James called and let Dante know everything was under control. Dante told Gage everything was ready, and then he waited until the G-Wagen was pulling back in front of the house. As Dante got out, he told Gage to hang out inside the Benz and let him know when he saw Gator pull up.

Dante exited the G-Wagen and entered the front gate of the house as Gage drove off. Dante then stepped onto the front porch as the front door swung open and Kyree stood there with a small smile on his lips.

"I had Robin call Gator," Kyree told Dante as he walked into the house. "He's on his way here now."

Dante saw the four women and one man all seated inside the front room with James standing next to them, leaning against the wall with his arms folded across his chest. Dante then looked at the group of five for a few moments.

"Which one of you is Robin?" Dante asked.

After a few moments in which nobody spoke up, Dante slowly began to smirk.

"I tell you what, if I have to ask again, I'll just start bodying one of you every time I have to ask," Dante threatened.

"Alright," Robin spoke up, seeing the well-known face as he began pulling out a chrome and gold gun from his shoulder holster under his left arm. "I'm Robin. Why are you here?"

Dante stared at the light-skinned female who was actually cute looking.

"This isn't about you or your friends, but it is about your boyfriend or whoever he is to you. I won't lie to you, I'm going to kill Gator!"

"What about us?" Robin asked Dante. "Whatever you and Gator got going on don't have nothing to do with us."

"Who are—?" Dante began, but then paused when he heard his cell phone go off. He looked at it and saw that it was Gage calling. "Yeah?"

"He just pulled up, Dante."

* * *

Gator hung up his phone as he walked from the driveway to the front door. Gator dug out his house key and was just reaching up to the door when it slowly swung open for him.

"What the fuck are you doing here?" Gator started to say after seeing Kyree at the front door.

He paused when he felt the familiar feeling of something pressing against the back of his head.

"Come on inside," Kyree told Gator with a smile as he stepped aside to allow both Gator and a gun-wielding Gage into the house. "Someone's here who wants to meet you."

Gator entered the house and first saw his family and his lady friends all sitting in the front room. He then noticed the white boy, before he locked eyes with the same man who not only ran the entire city of Miami's underworld but also had powerful people working for him.

"Welcome home!" Dante stated, smirking as he stared straight at Gator.

* * *

Alinna left the hospital and returned to the mansion, where she got Lisa to come back with her. Alinna had one of the servants bring everyone something to drink, and then she sat down beside Vanessa. Vanessa was on the phone with Dre, who still could not reach Dante on the phone.

"Lisa, are you okay?" Natalie asked her, watching the young woman from across the room. "Eddie's going to be okay."

Alinna heard the intercom buzz throughout the front of the mansion. She looked up to see Rose walk over to the speaker that was on the wall at the entrance to the kitchen.

"It's Floyd, Alinna!" Rose told her, receiving an approving nod from Alinna to let him inside the front gate.

Alinna then turned her attention back to the others, only to hear Maxine and Keisha both call out to her. She looked over at the twins and saw the news and the reporter talking about a huge fire in the upper-class neighborhood over in Albany.

"Oh shit! Look!" Maxine cried, pointing at the television screen. "There are James and Gage."

"That is!" Alinna said, spotting both of her husband's bodyguards just as her cell phone began to ring. She picked it up from the coffee table and saw it was Dante. "Dante, where are you?"

"I'm on my way home in a little bit," he told her. "I just had to handle something."

"I know," Alinna told him. "We're watching the news now, Dante!"

"News?"

"Yeah, Dante! And you need to get James and Gage off the camera."

"I got it!" Dante replied. "I'ma be home in a little bit, Alinna."

Alinna shook her head as she hung up with her husband.

"Is Dante alright, Alinna?" Yasmine asked.

"He's on his way home, Yasmine," Alinna told her, shaking her head again as she thought about Dante and the things he was able to do.

TEN

Dante got a call from Diamond a day after the whole scene took place with Gator. He found out that Fish Man had once again left the city, leaving a message on Diamond's hotel message mail and saying nothing else. Dante repeated this message to Alinna and the others, letting the family know what Diamond had told him.

Dante then received a call from Lieutenant Lewis about an hour after Diamond called to report about Fish Man.

"What's up, Lieutenant?" Dante answered.

"Dante, I received the papers your DEA friend sent to me, and I've read them with the chief. Right now we can't do much with him, because your friends were suddenly burned inside their home and no one has been able to find the other one. So Detective Howard can't be tied in. My advice though is to keep an eye on him, and I'll help also."

"I'll do that, and thanks, Lieutenant!" Dante told her as he hung up the phone afterward.

Dante sat down on his bed after speaking with Lewis and

thought a few minutes, before he picked up his phone to call Monica.

"Yes, Dante!"

"Where are you, Monica?"

"On my way back to the office. Why?"

"I was wondering if you was ready to leave?"

"Leave? Where are we going now, boy?"

"I did promise you to fly out to Puerto Rico to find Angela, right?" Dante asked her. "You still have that information you found on Angela, right?"

"Of course!" Monica answered. "Are you serious, Dante?"

"Give me two days to get everything straightened out with Alinna and the family, and then we're out of here!"

"I'm ready when you are!"

After hanging up with a hyped-up Monica, Melody and Natalie rushed into the bedroom. But Dante could barely understand what either of them was saying.

"Whoa! I can't understand what you two are saying!"

"Baby, Alinna just called. They're at the hospital and some detective is stopping Alinna and the others from leaving the hospital with Eddie," Natalie explained to her husband.

"Call Lieutenant Lewis and tell her I said to meet me at the hospital," Dante told Natalie as he snatched up his keys and took off from the bedroom.

Dante was outside three minutes later jogging to the garage and hitting the remote to raise the doors. He hopped over the car door and dropped into his Bugatti, since the top was down. He started up the engine, and within seconds he was backing out of the garage and flying out to the front gate.

* * *

"Detective, as I've said before," Alinna was saying, only to get interrupted by the detective who introduced himself as Detective Howard.

She looked to her right as Vanessa was hanging up the phone.

"Dante's on his way now," Vanessa whispered into Alinna's ear.

"Detective," Alinna said again, raising her voice, "my mother-in-law is coming out here in a few minutes with a family member, and we need to have everything ready. I've told you we cannot help you with your questions and now we're leaving!"

"I'm not done talking to you!" Detective Howard barked, stepping in front of Alinna, just as an Asian woman swiftly stepped between the two of them.

"Detective, I ask that you allow us to leave now. Please!" Yasmine requested in a calm but strong voice while staring the detective directly into his eyes.

The detective was opening his mouth to respond nastily to the Asian woman, only to pause and swing his head around to his left when he heard the loud roar of a powerful engine. He then saw the black and orange Bugatti swing into the hospital parking lot.

"Here we go!" Harmony said, shaking her head when she saw Dante quickly hop out of his car.

"Dante!" Alinna called out.

Alinna was not surprised that Dante completely ignored her as he walked right up into the face of the detective.

"Is there a problem?" Dante asked in a low growl as he stared directly into the detective's eyes.

The detective stepped back after instantly recognizing Dante Blackwell himself, now standing face to face with him.

"Dante Blackwell, himself! Welcome to my city, you son of a—!" Detective Howard said with a small smile.

"Correction, you stupid muthafucka!" Dante stated, cutting off the detective. "This is my city, and I'm only giving you this warning once: Stay the fuck away from my wife and my family, or I promise you I will murder you and everyone that knows you! Are we understood?"

"Muthafucka, you're under arrest!" Detective Howard yelled as he grabbed Dante's arm.

However, the detective soon found himself on his knees with the same arm of the hand that touched Dante now bent backward behind his back. That was in addition to the twenty guns now pointing down at him.

* * *

"Shit!" Lieutenant Lewis cursed as soon as she turned her Jaguar into the parking lot at the Manhattan Hospital.

She slammed on her brakes, jumped out of the car, and rushed toward Dante's side.

"Dante, that's enough!" Lewis yelled, pushing through the crowd to stand beside him. "Dante! Let him go! I've got it now!" she continued as she grabbed his arm.

The lieutenant sighed once Dante released the detective. She then looked at the detective as he quickly stood to his feet, grabbed his arm, and stared hatefully at Dante.

"Detective Howard, I've got it from here!" Lewis said.

"This mutha—!"

"That's an order, Detective!" Lewis told him, cutting him off and receiving a nasty look before the he began to slowly step back and walk away while talking to himself.

Lieutenant Lewis shook her head as she stood watching Detective Howard climb into his car. Moments later he flew out of the parking lot of the hospital. Lewis turned to face Dante and saw him standing in front of Alinna and Yasmine. She stared at him for a moment and caught a glimpse of a different side of the young legend.

"Either deal with dude or I will, Lieutenant!" Dante told her, noticing she was watching him.

"Dante, calm down!" Lewis told him as she walked over to the group. "Don't do anything that will draw any more attention to you, like killing a police officer!"

"I can deal with it!" Dante replied, remembering Monica's ex-DEA husband. "Just deal with him or I will!"

"Dante!"

Dante heard his name and looked behind him to see his mother and Lisa, and Eddie in a wheelchair being pushed out of the hospital. Dante left Alinna and Yasmine and walked over to his mother and cousin while ignoring Lisa's mean mug she was giving him as he stopped beside Eddie's chair.

"What's up, youngin'? How you feeling?"

"How the hell do you think he's feeling?" Lisa asked with an attitude, rolling her eyes at Dante while mumbling something nasty under her breath.

Dante ignored his cousin and squatted down beside Eddie.

"Youngin', it's my fault this shit happened to you. I should have had you some backup out there other than the team you had with you."

"It's nothing!" Eddie replied, hearing Lisa sucking her teeth. He ignored his girl and continued, "Hey, I heard about how you handled that nigga Gator. Good looking out, my nigga!"

"I want you to get better," Dante told him. "Once you're ready, I got a team for you that'll watch ya back and hold shit down for you."

"Hold up!" Lisa yelled. "Eddie isn't about to—!"

"Lisa, chill!" Eddie told her, raising his voice while cutting her off. "You need to let me deal with this!"

Lisa sucked her teeth and rolled her eyes as she walked off and headed across the parking lot to Eddie's car.

Eddie shook his head while watching her. He looked back at Dante and saw the expression on his face. "It's cool, Dante, my nigga! She'll be a'ight once I'm outta this chair, but I'ma get at you once I'm back on my feet."

Dante shook up with Eddie and then turned to his mother and gave her kiss on her cheek. "I'll see you later, Momma!" he said.

"Alright, baby!" Brenda replied, smiling as she watched her son walk back to where both his wives stood with their friends.

* * *

Dante spoke with Lieutenant Lewis a few minutes as he listened as she promised to keep a watch on Detective Howard. He then gave his keys to Vanessa to drive the Bugatti while he rode with Alinna and Yasmine inside the new Rolls-Royce Wraith he gifted to Alinna. He then glanced over toward his mother as Jung held open the back door of her new Bentley Bentayga. He caught her eye and winked at her, causing her to smile as she climbed into the SUV-model Bentley.

Once the Rolls-Royce left the parking lot, followed by his mother's Bentley and the security team for Alinna, Dante turned his focus to Alinna. "I spoke with Monica. We're leaving for Puerto Rico in two days."

"Angela?" Alinna asked him.

"I gotta finish things with Angela and keep my word I gave to Monica!" Dante said while nodding his head.

"How long you plan on being there, Dante?" Alinna asked with a slight attitude.

Dante caught the attitude and tone of Alinna's voice, and he realized that his wife had a major problem with him dealing with Angela. Dante then called out to his wife to get her attention. "Relax, shorty! What I have in mind for Angela should have you smiling if nothing else! Relax!" he told her.

"Whatever, Dante! You still didn't answer my question, nigga!" Alinna told him, rolling her eyes at him.

Dante smirked at Alinna's attitude, which he felt made her even sexier. He even noticed Yasmine smiling and watching them. He then looked back over at Alinna and answered her question. "We won't be gone no longer than a month, shorty!"

ELEVEN

Alinna rode with Dante and Monica out to the airstrip so the two of them could make their flight out to deal with Angela, who was hiding out in Puerto Rico. Alinna spoke very little along the way. She still had strange feelings about Dante being anywhere near Angela, who was the mother of her husband's first child.

Once they arrived at the airstrip, Alinna saw Rafael's people waiting. She waited until the Rolls-Royce pulled to a stop and Yasmine climbed out of the Wraith. Alinna then climbed out as Dante came walking around from the other side of the car.

"Where's Monica?" Alinna asked as Vanessa, Amber, and a team of security walked up.

"She'll be here!" Dante replied while watching Rafael's boys walk over Angela's husband, Geno, to him, who looked better than when he last saw the man. "Let your boss know I owe him," he told Rafael's boys, handing one of the three guys a rolled knot of cash.

Dante received a nod from the guy he handed the cash to. He then shifted his eyes to Geno after the three Jamaican men walked off.

"Been a long time!" Dante said.

Geno looked up from staring at the ground to meet the one man he hated more than any person alive. He then started to spit into Dante's face, only to catch a glimpse of something fly past his eyes. Pain exploded from the right side of his face, and he found himself on all fours with blood flowing from his mouth.

"Keep your spit inside of your mouth," Yasmine told Geno, noticing him working up to spit at Dante.

Dante smirked as he looked over to Yasmine as she stood over Geno, who barely caught her movements before suddenly hitting the ground. Dante heard his name and looked over at Amber pointing at something. He looked in the direction she was pointing to see the metallic-black Benz truck turning onto the airstrip.

"What's Gomez doing here?" Alinna asked, also noticing the Benz truck.

Dante heard Alinna's question but chose not to answer her.

Instead, he turned back to Geno and told him to get up off the ground, just as Vanessa cried out, "Oh shit! Monica's fucking Gomez!"

Dante looked back over at the Benz truck to see Monica kissing Gomez. He slowly smirked, already aware of them seeing one another.

"Alright, you two! We gotta get going!" Dante stated.

Alinna looked at her husband and heard how calm he sounded and saw the smirk on his face. She balled up her face and stared at him.

"You knew about those two, didn't you?" she asked.

"Maybe!" Dante replied, winking his eye at Alinna and smirking as both Monica and Gomez walked up.

"You ready, boy?" Monica asked playfully, punching Dante in the stomach.

"Yeah!" Dante answered. "You got your handcuffs with you?"

Monica looked over to the guy beside Dante and recognized him as Geno. She pulled out her cuffs and began handcuffing him.

Dante turned back to Alinna as Monica took care of Geno.

Dante then kissed Alinna and then Yasmine. "I'ma call once we land in Puerto Rico. Stay out of trouble while I'm gone!"

"You just make sure you don't make me whoop your ass when you get back!" Alinna told him, kissing him again and then watching as he turned and started toward the G-4 with a smirk after hearing what she just told him.

Alinna watched as Dante and Monica disappeared inside the jet after Geno, and then continued watching until the jet was in the air. She then turned and walked back over to the Rolls-Royce.

"Alinna, are you okay?" Yasmine asked, once she and Alinna were inside the back of the Wraith and leaving the airstrip.

Alinna shook her head and remained quiet a moment while staring out the window. She started to answer Yasmine, just as her phone began ringing. She saw it was Tony T calling on the other line. "Yeah, Tony."

"Alinna, where's Dante?"

"You just missed him, Tony. Why?"

"We got a problem. We just got word that this Cuban muthafucka just got in town and is looking for Dante about money that's owed to him."

"Money!" Alinna repeated, but began chuckling. "Find out this Cuban's contact number. I'll deal with him."

* * *

Dante got a little rest on the flight to Puerto Rico, but he spent most of the time talking with Monica and reading over the papers she had on Angela. He then focused most of his attention on what he was reading, but became aware of the jet beginning its descent.

"Dante, we're close!" Monica announced to him.

Dante was ready once the G-4 landed and the hatch was opened. He escorted Geno off the jet and spotted the sixty-four-inch Maybach waiting with a chauffeur.

"I thought we was going to blend in, Dante?" Monica asked as she, Dante, and Geno started toward the car.

"We are!" he replied in a clueless voice.

"Dante!" Monica said, getting him to look over at her. "How the hell are we supposed to blend in riding in a May-damn-bach?"

After climbing into the back of the Maybach, after nodding to the chauffeur and sitting Geno on the left side, Dante waited until the driver shut the door.

"You wanna start looking for Angela tonight or in the morning?" Dante asked.

"What about him?" Monica asked, nodding over to Geno.

"We can either take him with us or leave his ass at the hotel. Choose!"

Monica shook her head at Dante and then rolled her eyes at him and motioned for the driver to let him know they were going to their hotel. She then looked back at Dante.

"How exactly do you plan on keeping him locked up at the hotel, Dante?"

Dante slowly smiled a demented-looking smirk as he looked over at Monica. "I'm sure you know I can think of a few ways to keep him at the hotel," Dante said.

"You really are insane, boy!" Monica told him, shaking her head and smiling at him.

* * *

"Hello!"

Alinna heard a thick Spanish accent from the deep voice that answered the phone.

"I was told you were looking for Dante Blackwell

concerning the matters of missing money and Fish Man?" Alinna said.

"Who is this?"

"Alinna Blackwell. Dante Blackwell's wife. What can I do for you, Mr. Francisco?"

"You can do nothing for me, woman! I want to talk to this bastard Dante Blackwell! He owes me a lot of money, and I want to know who do he think he is! This is my city, and this black son of a—!"

"Mr. Francisco," Alinna spoke up, cutting off the Cuban drug boss, "I'll say this to you and then I'll end this conversation: You're very lucky to be dealing with me instead of my husband, because after the first words of disrespect that spilled out of your mouth, this phone call would have ended and my husband would have been on his way to see you. I am going to say this one last time. This city, as well as New Jersey, no longer belongs to you! These two cities belong to the Blackwell family now. And as for whatever money you mentioned that is owed to you, I think you need to take it as a loss, because neither my husband nor myself will be leaving this city nor will we be paying you anything! It was nice speaking with you and goodbye!"

After hanging up on the Cuban, Alinna looked to the others who were sitting around listening for her to get off the phone.

"What's up, Alinna?" Dre asked her. "We warring or what?"

"I'm pretty sure this Garcia guy isn't going to let the way I just spoke to him just slide, so I want everybody on point and ready for anything to happen," Alinna warned.

"Are you going to let Dante know about this, Alinna?" Natalie asked her, just as Brenda spoke up.

"We all know how my son is. If we tell Dante about this issue, we all know he will be back in New York within hours. My advice is that we not overreact and tell Dante until it's completely necessary. We should be capable of dealing with this ourselves. Dre, Tony T, and the other men can maintain security, and Yasmine can stay close to Alinna with a team of security. Are we in agreement?"

Alinna stared at her husband's mother while everyone else sat or stood and waited for Alinna's response. She sat thinking the whole plan over in her mind, but eventually gave in. "Alright. We can hold off on contacting Dante about this, but everybody needs to stay ready at all times. Period!"

* * *

Alinna finally received the call she was waiting for. She lay in bed with her sleeping son talking to her husband.

"So, how's everything going there so far?"

"We've gone by the address Monica had, but nobody lives there. Monica's going to look somewhere elsc. She's going to contact Nash Johnson back there and have him look into a few things for us as well."

"You try seeing if Geno knows anything?"

"He won't talk; and when I was going to make his ass, Monica wouldn't let me mess with him."

"So you two basically are just out there with nothing right now, huh?" she asked, watching Natalie walk into the bedroom with baby Damian in her arms.

"Is that Dante?" Natalie asked as she was laying Damian down in his baby bed.

Alinna told Dante to hold on as she handed the phone to Natalie to talk with him. Alinna then picked up her son and carried Dante Jr. from the bedroom to his own room that he shared with Andre Jr. She laid her son down and then covered him and kissed his cheek. Alinna kissed her nephew and left both Dante Jr. and Andre Jr.'s bedroom and headed back to her own bedroom.

While walking back into the bedroom, Alinna saw that Yasmine was now on the phone with Dante. Alinna simply smiled as she walked over to the bed and climbed back inside to lie down. She ended up waiting another five minutes until Yasmine handed her back the phone.

"Yeah, baby!" Alinna said into the phone as she broke out into a smile at the smooth, mildly deep sound of Dante's voice.

TWELVE

By their fourth day in San Juan, Dante and Monica had looked all over the area, when they finally hit the jackpot, after Nash finally got back to them with two new addresses.

They tried the first of the two addresses, which actually led to a meeting with Angela's relatives. They met Angela's mother and two sisters, who instantly recognized him from pictures Angela had shown them. After they spent some time with her family, they made up a lie that he was there to surprise her, and Dante then got them to agree not to say anything to Angela. Dante also came up with a third address and even a phone number. After saying their goodbyes and receiving hugs from Angela's family, both Dante and Monica walked out to the car.

"So what now?" Monica asked, once they got back inside the Maybach.

"We see how accurate this number is first," Dante stated as he pulled out the cell phone he bought once in Puerto Rico.

He called the number Angela's mother gave him and then sat and listened to the ringing until someone picked up on the end.

"Hello!"

Dante instantly recognized Angela's voice with her Cuban accent he knew so well. Dante then simply hung up the phone and smiled.

"Let me guess!" Monica stated after Dante hung up the phone. "That's an accurate number, isn't it?"

"Yes, it's accurate," Dante answered, just as the cell phone rang in his hand.

He looked at the phone screen and saw Brenda was calling him.

"Yeah, Momma!"

"Dante, it's Vanessa," she replied. "Dante, it's Alinn— she's been kidnapped!"

* * *

Within twenty minutes Dante was already in the air, leaving Monica at the airstrip in Puerto Rico. As Dante made the flight from San Juan back to New York, he tried to remain calm while he thought over and over what Vanessa had told him about Alinna. He wasn't even aware of his own tears running down his face, and he was too pissed to even care.

Once he landed back in New York, he wasted no time rushing off the G-4, to see Vanessa and Dre waiting for him.

"What the fuck happened to my wife?" he barked as he walked up to the Hummer.

Vanessa and Dre kept quiet and just stared at him.

"I don't give a fuck what happened! But I promise if anything happens to Alinna, I'ma murder the muthafucka responsible and then each muthafucka that knew about this bullshit and allowed it to happen! Now get me the fuck outta here!" Dante said.

* * *

Alinna slowly opened her eyes, but she had problems seeing out of her left eye. She tried to reach for her face, but she quickly realized she could not since she was tied to a chair. She looked around with her good eye and saw she was in a dimly lit room. She then thought how cold she seemed to feel, and only then did she realize she was completely naked.

Alinna remembered the young woman who was responsible for her being in her current situation. She then promised herself that if she got out of the mess, she was going to kill the woman who had set her up.

Alinna heard the room door being unlocked and tried to look over with her good eye. She saw the door open and in walk a six-foot-one, 230-pound Cuban man. He was followed by a woman, who was the one responsible for setting her up. They were followed by a middle-aged Cuban man wearing a gray suit.

"I see you've finally decided to wake!" Garcia Francisco said, smiling down at Alinna. "I was beginning to tire of waiting on you. But since you're awake now, maybe we can finish our conversation we were having before you rudely hung up the phone on me!"

"How about you kiss my ass!" Alinna told the Cuban drug boss before looking over at the woman. "And as for you, I will kill you, bitch! You have no idea who the fuck you crossed! I will kill you myself!"

Alinna barely finished what she had to say when the big man on her left open-hand slapped her across the face, sending both blood and spit flying. Alinna could taste the blood in her mouth, but she smiled as she looked at the big man.

"I'll make sure I personally introduce you to my husband. I'm sure Dante will love to know who's responsible for my face looking like this!"

"Where is this Dante Blackwell?" Garcia Francisco spoke up again.

Alinna looked back at the Cuban and slowly smiled. "I'll give you a clue on how to find my husband. Just listen to the screaming, since I'm sure he knows who's crossed his family!"

* * *

"Lieutenant Lewis?" Dante asked to make sure he had heard Yasmine correctly. "Yasmine, you sure it was the lieutenant?"

Yasmine slowly nodded her head, but she was unable to meet Dante's eyes after failing him and allowing Alinna to be taken.

"They were supposed to meet, my husband. The lieutenant said she had information about both Fish Man and the Cuban drug lord Garcia Francisco; and once we met, I allowed Alinna to join the lieutenant inside of her vehicle. Alinna was only inside with the lieutenant for a moment when everything began happening fast. Three cars showed up and blocked me inside my parking space while the lieutenant sped off!" Yasmine softly explained.

"Did you see which way they went, Yasmine?" Dante asked, trying to remain calm throughout everything but feeling the fire burning in his chest from the anger and even fear that was building inside of him.

"I didn't see!" Yasmine answered as tears began falling down her face while staring down at the ground.

Dante shook his head and tried to think. He had to calm himself down more to finally begin to come up with a plan.

"Somebody give me a phone!" Dante ordered.

Dante took Melody's phone and looked over at his mother as she stood with Dwayne.

"Momma, what's the chief's number? I've gotta plan that may work."

* * *

"What exactly are you planning to do with her?" Lieutenant Megan Lewis asked her employer, standing inside the office at Garcia's mansion.

"She'll receive the same as the husband," Garcia told her. "We will find and deal with Dante Blackwell. But before he dies, he will watch his wife die in front of him, and then he will die behind her, with her death new in his mind."

"Mr. Francisco," Lewis started, before she was interrupted by the ringing of her phone. She then held up her finger for Garcia to hold on as she pulled out her phone to see that her chief was calling her. "Yeah, Chief!"

"Lewis, where are you?" Chief Grant asked in a loud voice. "I need you for a case to back up Sergeant Jones! How soon can you get to 135th and Queen Bridge?"

"Give me twenty minutes, Chief!" Lewis told her boss, hanging up the phone and then walking back over to Garcia, who was now on the phone himself.

"You're leaving?" Garcia asked the lieutenant, laying his desk phone onto his chest.

Lewis explained to him that she had a problem to handle, but told him that she'd return later once she was done. She then rushed out of the office.

* * *

Chief Patrick Grant called back the number that contacted him, once he hung up with Lieutenant Lewis. He sat at his desk and listened as the line rang.

"Yeah!"

"She's on her way now. It should take her twenty minutes."

"I'll have $1,000,000 wired to your account by tomorrow morning!"

Chief Grant smiled after Dante Blackwell hung up the phone. He remained smiling when he thought about the

$1,000,000 he was going to receive for giving up Lieutenant Lewis.

* * *

Lieutenant Lewis turned onto Queens Bridge exactly twenty-one minutes after leaving Garcia Francisco's mansion. She looked around in a confused state, and saw nothing and no sergeant around. She slowed her Jaguar to a stop while she pulled out her cell phone.

Lewis called the chief back to find out where Sergeant Jones was. She heard the line ring only once, when she saw the streets light up. Two SUVs drew her attention away from the phone as they pulled up in front of her and blocked her in. She then looked back behind her to see two more SUVs block her off from the backside as well.

"What the hell!" Lewis cried out as she tried to turn back and face forward, only to freeze as her eyes locked on the guy who was climbing out of the Mercedes-Benz G-Wagen.

Lewis swung her head around to her door after it was snatched open. She barely got a scream off, when she was grabbed from the Jaguar and then slammed back against the car door.

"What the hell do—?" Lewis stated but quickly paused in

the middle of what she was just saying when Dante Blackwell himself stepped in front of her.

"Where is my wife?" Dante asked in a voice just above a whisper, staring the lieutenant directly in her eyes.

"Dante, what are you—?"

Lewis was unable to finish her sentence. Dante kicked her right leg out from under her, and she felt herself falling back. She then felt a horrible pain explode in her face, after it was slammed into the driver's side window.

Dante released the lieutenant and watched her as she dropped to the ground to her knees, holding her broken nose with blood pouring out.

"Get up!" Dante said with no emotion.

Lewis slowly rose to her feet, only to be snatched up and shoved back against the car door again. She cut her eyes over toward Dante's best friend and brother, Dre, and met his eyes, which were as hateful as Dante's. She then looked back to Dante.

"Where's my wife?" he asked again.

"Dante, I don't know!"

Dante grabbed Lewis's face in his hand while she was talking again but not saying what he wanted to hear. He then slammed her head so hard into the driver's window this time that he smashed her head clean through, breaking the glass window. He then heard her crying out for mercy, promising to tell him what he wanted to know.

* * *

Garcia was impressed with the strength and resilience of the young Puerto Rican woman as he stood watching her take and deal with as much as his bodyguard Pablo could give her. He first beat her with his fist, and then he switched to a leather belt after wetting her body all over. Garcia stood watching the beating a little while longer before he finally spoke up and told Pablo to stop.

Garcia then walked over to stand in front of Alinna as he called her name. He was a little surprised that she still showed signs of cockiness, even after the pain Pablo had put her through.

"So, Mrs. Blackwell, are you ready to tell me where your husband is, or should we continue?"

"Muthafucka! You can kiss my—!" Alinna started, but stopped in the middle of what she was saying as she and Garcia and his lynch man jumped in surprise at the sudden explosion and screams.

Alinna heard the sounds of guns going off, more explosions, and louder screams. She slowly began to smile when she realized Dante was finally there. She looked to the Cuban drug boss and met his eyes. "You was looking for my husband. Well, he found you!" she joked.

* * *

Dante moved through the mansion like death itself. He spared nothing and no one. Everyone he aimed his SK submachine gun at turned into fallen bodies. He followed the lieutenant's directions as he continued moving through the mansion, aware that James, Gage, and Dre were all close by. He then turned down another corner just in time to see a team of three gunmen running in his direction.

Brrrrrrr! Brrrrrrr!

Dante chopped up the three would-be gunmen. After hearing the clicking that announced the SK was empty, he then dropped the gun and pulled out one of his .40s from his left holster, just as Dre caught up to him.

"You good?" Dre asked, looking down at the three bodies in front of him and Dante.

"Not until I get Alinna back!" Dante replied as he once again went on the hunt.

* * *

"Just pick up the bitch!" Garcia yelled as he started for the door as Pablo grabbed a struggling and fighting Alinna, who continued yelling.

Garcia led Pablo from the basement and back up the stairs. He then looked around before stepping out into the hallway and making it out front just as another young man and a huge muscular guy holding an AR-15 in his hands stepped out in front of the mansion.

"Dante!" Alinna screamed after seeing her husband and beginning to struggle and fight harder to get away from Garcia's man.

"Put her down!" Dante demanded with a growl, all while walking toward Garcia. "Now!"

"So, this is the famous Dante Blackwell!" Garcia started but paused at the swiftness the young legend had when he pulled out his chrome and gold gun and pointed it directly at Garcia's face.

"So, you plan on killing me? Pablo will kill your wife if you try!" Garcia said with a sinister smile.

Boom! Boom!

Garcia jumped in both surprise and shock at the sudden

explosion from the cannon inside Dante's hand. Garcia opened his eyes and quickly became aware of two things: One was that Dante suddenly had two chrome and gold guns in his hands, and the second was that Pablo was screaming in pain. He cut his eyes over to his bodyguard to see Pablo on the ground with both his knees blown out.

"Dre!" Dante yelled. "Get Alinna outta here!"

Dante stared directly into the eyes of the Cuban drug lord as Dre gently picked up Alinna after first untying her and then pulling off his T-shirt and putting it on her. Dante then waited until the two of them were gone.

"So, you was looking for me, and since you couldn't find me, you grabbed my wife, huh?" Dante said.

"This was about—!"

"You should have done your homework better," Dante continued. "You was better off coming after me than the woman you did. I will go up against Satan himself when it comes to that woman, and you've crossed the one line no man should ever cross!"

"It was my—!"

Boom!

"Agghhhh!" Garcia yelled out in extreme pain, hitting the

ground and grabbing his right knee after Dante blew it off.

Dante ignored the yelling coming from both men laid out in front of him. He then looked at his custom-made Mickey Mouse rose gold and diamond-bezel watch and saw that he had five minutes left.

Boom!

Dante blew out Garcia's other knee and continued to ignore the screaming. He then simply turned and left the room and headed toward the front of the mansion.

* * *

Chief Grant hung up the phone after receiving a call from the mayor about the war zone in the southeast side of Long Island. He was already watching the news coverage on the blown-up mansion and the large number of bodies that were all over the streets.

Grant reached for his personal cell phone on his left when it began ringing.

"Hello?" the chief answered when he saw who was calling.

"Everything's finished!"

Chief Grant recognized Dante's voice and then focused on the phone call.

"I'm looking at the news report now. Is your wife okay?"

"She'll be okay!"

"I take it that Garcia Francisco isn't a problem anymore after what was shown on the news, correct?"

"I'll have someone wire the money to whatever account you want it sent to. Just let me know by tonight's end; and I'm going to need a contact that you would trust yourself chief. I'm only asking because my mother trusts you!"

"I'll take care of it!" Chief Grant told Dante, only to hear the call end with Dante hanging up the phone.

THIRTEEN

D ante relaxed with Alinna while she went through the whole healing process. They spent time away from the family after she was released from the hospital, and rented out a penthouse in a hotel in Staten Island. Dante waited on his wife hand and foot, taking care of her. They both enjoyed every moment of their time together.

Dante had received word from Monica through Vanessa that Angela had remarried a businessman in San Juan and that she had her own business. She was also doing surprisingly well as a private investigator. Dante sent a message back to Monica letting her know not to interfere with Angela just yet, but that she could either come back to the States or remain in Puerto Rico until he returned there himself.

After three weeks of just relaxing and allowing Alinna to get better, both Dante and she decided it was time to head back to the mansion with the family. Alinna was missing her son, only talking to him over the phone, and Dante wanted to get back to business. They left the hotel in Dante's Bugatti and headed toward Buffalo. Alinna looked over at Dante, and for a few moments she just sat watching him.

"What's on your mind, shorty?" Dante asked, noticing out of the corner of his eye Alinna was staring at him.

"Dante, I wanna go home!" Alinna told him. "I mean go home!"

Dante took his eyes from the road a brief moment to look at Alinna, meeting her eyes for that moment.

"A'ight! We can leave whenever you're ready, shorty!" Dante said as he focused back on the road.

"Tonight!" Alinna told him.

"Tonight it is then!" Dante said with a nod of his head.

* * *

They arrived back at the mansion a little while later to find everyone home. Dante parked the Bugatti in front of the front door and then got out and walked around to open Alinna's door for her.

"Momma!"

Alinna turned around when she heard and recognized her son's voice. She broke out in a smile to see Dante Jr. rushing toward her. She braced herself since she was still a little sore, only for Dante to intercept his son, snatching him up off his feet and out of his charge at his mother.

"Slow down, lil' man!" Dante told his son. "Your mom's a little sore still, so be gentle with her."

Alinna smiled at Dante in thanks, and then she turned to Dante Jr. and held out her arms to him. "Come give me a hug, D.J.!"

Dante smiled as he watched his wife and son. He then looked up as the rest of the family walked in. Mya threw her arms around her father's waist in a hug.

"You two finally decided to come home, huh?" Vanessa said as she waited while Natalie and Yasmine hugged Dante, before she hugged and kissed her brother.

"Where are Wesley and Amber at?" Dante asked with a smile.

Dante then noticed his mother stepping out of the front door, with Dwayne following behind. Dante then left the group a second and walked over to hug his mother and kiss her on the cheek. He then nodded to his mother's husband, who nodded back at him.

"How is she?" Brenda asked Dante, looking over at her

daughter-in-law and seeing her face still had some bruises, but looking a great deal better than she had.

"She's still a little sore around her body, but she's a lot better than she was!" Dante told his mother.

Just then, Alinna looked directly at him and smiled. He winked his eye and smiled back at her.

* * *

Once everyone was inside the mansion and in the den, Dante noticed that not only were Wesley and Amber missing but also Lisa and Eddie.

"Where are Wesley, Amber, Lisa, and Eddie?" he asked out loud.

"Wesley and Amber went back to Phoenix, and they invited Lisa and Eddie to go with them," Harmony told Dante while she was sitting next to Alinna.

"Well, we got some news also!" Dante stated to the family. "Alinna wants to go home. I'm taking her back to Miami, and since we've got control of both New York and New Jersey, we'll switch up things a little with our plan. Vanessa and Dre can still get settled out in New Jersey, but I'ma need Tony T and Harmony out here in New York so I can get Alinna back home.

"What about Fish Man, fam?" Tony T asked Dante.

"I've been thinking about that!" Dante admitted. "I'm going to dead that issue for now, since the nigga's punk ass is running again. But if he shows up at any point, I want to know. His ass is dead. Period!"

"So you're leaving then?" Brenda asked her son, drawing Dante's attention to her.

Dante stared at his mother and then said, "Momma, I want you, Dwayne, and Melody to come back to Miami with us. I can give you the penthouse or buy you a house, whichever you all want. I'll even let you guys open another business in Miami. We already own a night club, so another business wouldn't hurt."

"Dante, we've allowed you to do enough for us as it is, Son!" Dwayne spoke up, when normally he remained quiet when Dante and Brenda dealt with one another. "As a man, Dante, I wouldn't feel right continuing to allow you to do for my family and not repay you for it!"

"Alright, Dwayne," Dante began, staring him in the eyes. "Momma told me you're into driving trucks. You got your

CDLs right?"

"Sure do!"

"Well, how 'bout me and you opening a truck business?" Dante asked Dwayne. "You'll run everything, and I'll be a silent partner. What do you think?"

Dwayne was surprised and not expecting the offer his wife's son had just made him. He looked at Brenda and met her eyes and smiled. Dwayne then looked back at Dante and saw the young man waiting and watching him.

"You say I'll run the business, right?"

"I'll just be the silent partner!" Dante repeated to his mother's husband.

"Alright, Son. You've got a deal!" Dwayne said with a smile and a shake of his head.

Dante smiled as he and Dwayne shook hands. He then looked over at his mother and saw her smiling and looking over in his direction. He winked at her and received a kiss that Brenda blew back at him.

* * *

Dante wasted little time packing up what they needed and wanted to take with them. They decided to leave Emmy for

Tony T and Harmony to look after. Dante had Natalie arrange everything with having the G-Wagen, Bugatti, Rolls-Royce Wraith, and the BMW M6 shipped down to Miami. He was out front with James and Gage, talking with Dre and Tony T when Alinna and the others all exited out the front door of the mansion.

"Boy, you better give me a hug before you leave!" Vanessa told Dante, already tearing up as she rushed to her brother, throwing her arms around his neck and hugging him tightly.

"I'ma miss you, big brother!"

"Come on, baby girl!" Dante said as he held Vanessa and kissed her cheek. "You know where I'ma be at, and if you need me, I'm wherever you at. I promise."

"I love you, Dante," Vanessa told him, kissing his cheek and hugging him tightly again.

Dante, Alinna, and the others all said their goodbyes, and then Gage drove one of the Escalades escorting everyone out to the airstrip where the G-4 was waiting for them. They arrived at the airstrip five minutes later and parked, leaving the SUV for Tony T to have someone pick up later on. Dante walked with his family while security grabbed their bags. He nodded to their personal pilot, who was well taken care of by the family. Dante then led his family onto the G-4 jet.

"Dante!" Rose called to her employer and the young man who she long ago considered her son.

"Yeah, Rose?" he answered as he sat down beside his friend. "You okay?"

"I'm wonderful, baby," Rose answered as she patted Dante's thigh and smiled at him. "I just wanted to speak with you about Dante Jr. and Mya a few minutes."

"What happened?" he asked, with a concerned look on his face.

He glanced over to where both Dante Jr. and Mya were sitting with Natalie and playing with their brother, Damian.

"Those babies are wonderful, Dante!" Rose told him. "But I've helped raise those babies, and that Dante Jr. is an extremely bright boy, just as his sister is. I understand you may not want to put those babies in school because of the lifestyle you and Alinna live, but I think it would be good to at least give them home-schooling, Dante. They need it!"

Dante nodded his head after listening to what Rose had to tell him. He quickly agreed with her suggestion.

"I'll get with Alinna and we'll get right on it, Rose."

"Thank you, sweety," Rose told Dante, just as Mya and Dante Jr. came rushing over to him and Rose.

* * *

They landed at the airstrip in Miami a few hours later and were not surprised to see Greg Wilson already waiting for them with Dante's Bentley and Alinna's Phantom. There were three Cadillac Escalades waiting as well. Dante was the first one off the jet, along with James and Gage on each side of him.

"Welcome back!" Greg Wilson said with a smile as he shook hands with Dante.

"It's actually good to be home!" Dante replied, just as Alinna, Yasmine, and Natalie all walked up.

"Hey, Wilson!" Alinna said, smiling at the sight of their family friend.

"How you feeling, Alinna?" he asked, smiling at her and seeing that she was looking much better than the way Dante had explained to him after the kidnapping and beating. "I'm happy you all decided to come home. I actually like you all!"

"Don't let me know you're getting soft on us, Wilson!" Dante jokingly said to his friend and personal private detective.

He then introduced his mother, Dwayne, and Melody to Greg.

"Hello, Greg," Melody said with a smile.

"Wilson!" Dante called. "I need a favor."

"I'm already expecting it!" Wilson admitted jokingly. "What's up, Dante?"

Dante explained to Greg what he wanted him to do concerning finding a location and at least six to ten trucks to start up the business he and Dwayne were going to start up.

"I'll get started right on that!" Wilson replied as he handed Dante the keys to the Escalade. "I also got a call from a Betty White about a Bugatti, a Rolls-Royce Wraith, and some other cars like a G-Wagen. I see you all bought new toys while out of town!"

"Blame Natalie and Alinna!" Dante told him as he handed Yasmine the keys to the Escalades for security.

Dante then led his mother, Dwayne, and Melody over to his Bentley and introduced them all to his armed chauffeur who was Alinna's personal driver. However, Dante decided to assign him to his mother, her husband, and Melody for a while.

After saying their goodbyes to Greg Wilson, Dante waited

until his wives were inside the Phantom and both Gage and James were in the front seat.

"Dante, where's Rose and the kids?" Alinna asked as she leaned in against him.

"I sent them with my mom and Melody," Dante answered as he dug out a box of Black & Milds.

"My husband!" Yasmine called to Dante, getting his attention. "Monica phoned before we left New York, and Harmony called the phone inside the jet while you were asleep. Monica wants you to call her as soon as possible."

"She say what it's about?" Dante asked as Natalie got comfortable against him on his other side.

"Just that you needed to call her soon because it was about Angela!" Yasmine told her husband, watching as he pulled out his cell phone from his pocket.

After finding the contact number he had for Monica in Puerto Rico, Dante listened to the phone ring and ring, until the voice mail picked up. He hung up the phone and tried calling again, only to receive Monica's voice mail again.

* * *

Once they reached their mansion and parked out front,

Dante and the girls climbed out of the Phantom as Brenda and the others got out of the Bentley.

"Oh my God, Dante! This is just as big as the one back in New York!" Brenda cried in amazement, looking around at her son's home.

Alinna smiled at Dante's mother and then looked over at him and said, "I'll be happy to show them around."

Dante nodded his head and smirked while looking over at his mother. He received kisses from Alinna, Natalie, and Yasmine as the three of them left his side and walked over to his mother, sister, and Dwayne and went inside.

"It's actually good to be home!" James stated with a smile as he looked around the mansion's front grounds.

"James!" Alinna called out as soon as he, Dante, and Gage entered the front door. "You've got a phone call!" she said as she handed him the phone.

"Who is it?" James asked, mouthing the question.

"Maxine!" Alinna replied, with a little laugh as James took the phone.

James shook his head, but saw Dante and Gage watching him and smirking. He then left the front of the mansion and walked into the kitchen area where Rose and the kids were all eating lunch.

"What's up, Max?" James asked, after placing the phone to his ear.

"I'll be there by 6:30 p.m. tonight. Pick me up from the airstrip, James."

"You flying here?"

"Yes I am. Why?"

"What about Keisha? You're not staying up there with her?"

"My man is in Miami, so I'm flying to Miami to be with you, unless you've changed your mind about being with me. Is that it, James?"

"I'll be out at the airstrip, Max."

"I love you!"

"Love you too, Max!" James told her, sighing and shaking his head.

"So I guess you're letting Mari go?" Dante said to him from behind.

James jumped up and spun around to see both Dante and Gage standing a few feet behind him still smirking.

142

"Mari decided she just wanted to go back to Phoenix," James answered, but then added, "I care about Mari, but for some crazy reason, I'm in love with Maxine's crazy ass!"

"So she's coming here?" Gage asked him.

James nodded his head in response to Gage's question.

"Maxine's also pregnant!" James added.

"Who's pregnant?" Alinna asked as she and Melody walked into the kitchen, catching the ending of what James was saying.

"James and Maxine!" Dante told her, cutting his eyes back to James and still smirking at his boy.

"Oh my God! James!" Alinna cried happily as she rushed over to him and threw her arms around him in a hug. "I'm so happy for you and Maxine. But why didn't she come back with us if she's having your baby?"

"She's flying out here now!" James informed Alinna.

"We have to throw her a baby shower!" Melody excitedly jumped in.

"That sounds like a good idea," Alinna said in agreement. "What's Maxine's new number, James?"

James gave Alinna her new cell phone number and then

shook his head. He looked over and watched as she and Melody walked off talking to each other. He then looked back at Dante and Gage and saw them both smirking, which soon turned into them laughing at him.

FOURTEEN

Monica sat across the street from the mini-mansion where Angela and her new husband lived. She sat and waited for Angela to leave the house and drive her S63 Mercedes-Benz, which was parked in front and still running, with the driver's door wide open. Monica patiently waited until the front door swung open and Angela walked outside, followed by her husband who remained at the door watching his wife rush off.

"I'm impressed!" Monica said, looking from Angela's husband to Angela as she was climbing inside of the Benz. "Follow the Mercedes, Harry!" she told the chauffeur while she continued to stare at the Benz as Angela pulled off.

Monica insisted that the chauffeur not get too close to the Benz as she began forming a simple plan when the Benz pulled up to a red light.

"Pull up beside the Mercedes," she told her driver. "Wait for me!" she added, once the Maybach was beside the Benz.

Monica climbed out of the back of the Maybach while

pulling her Glock 19 from her side holster hidden behind her leather jacket. She walked right up to the driver's door of the Benz and tapped on the glass.

"Open the door!" Monica told Angela, who turned and looked out the window.

Monica ignored the look that appeared on Angela's face.

"Get out!" Monica yelled, after snatching open the car door once Angela didn't move to open the door herself.

She just sat in the car in complete shock and surprise. Monica then forcefully grabbed her and then pushed Angela toward the Maybach.

"Wh-What are you doing here?" Angela asked once she got control of herself.

She stopped at the back door of the Maybach, only to spin around to face Monica and the Glock 19 that was now pointing directly at her face.

"You ask one more question or do anything other than what I've told you to do, and I will kill you. Now get into the car. Now!"

Angela did as she was told and turned to climb into the back of the Maybach, only to feel herself get pushed up against the car and handcuffed.

"What the hell?" Angela began, but quickly stopped at the press of Monica's gun to the side of her ribs.

"Get the hell inside the car, Angela!" Monica demanded.

* * *

Dante stood outside the front of the mansion with James, Gage, and Dwayne. They were all waiting for Alinna and the rest of the women to come outside. They were going to go out to eat dinner as a family. Dante stood listening with both James and Gage as Dwayne told them the story about how he met Brenda. Dante heard his cell phone wake up, ringing from inside his pocket, just as the front door opened and Alinna and the other women walked out the door. Dante dug out his phone as he walked up and shut and locked the front door.

"What's up, Mon—?"

"Dante, where are you?" Monica asked, cutting him off once he answered the phone.

"Monica, what's up?" Dante asked, stopping in mid-step, with his face balled up from the tone of Monica's voice.

"Dante, just tell me where the hell you are!" Monica demanded, almost close to yelling into the phone.

"Monica, I'm back in Miami!" Dante answered calmly. "What's going on?"

"Dante, I'm on my way to the airstrip. Have someone there for me when I get there. I'm bringing gifts!"

* * *

Monica climbed into the G-4 that belonged to Dante and his wives as she hung up with Dante. She escorted both Angela and her first husband, Geno, onto the jet. She sat them both down a few seats apart and handcuffed them to their seats.

Monica then took a seat and sighed as she sat back. She shut her eyes for a moment, only to re-open them and look at Angela, who asked Monica if she was now working for Dante.

"My advice, Angela: Don't talk to me or you won't make it to Miami!" Monica told the ex-captain in a calm but serious-toned voice.

Angela decided to ignore Monica before she ended up killing her then and there. Instead, she shut her eyes and once again relaxed her mind.

* * *

The plane landed at the airstrip in Miami a couple hours later, waking up Monica from her light sleep when she felt the plane landing. She then uncuffed Angela and Geno from the seats and re-cuffed their hands behind their backs. Monica then escorted the two to the G-4's hatch as the pilot opened up the door.

"Why am I not surprised!" Angela stated as soon as she stepped off the jet and saw Dante himself along with Alinna and friends.

Angela made her way down the stairs behind her ex-husband, to whom she was actually still legally married. She couldn't help but stare at Dante in his silk Armani suit. She was unable to deny how handsome he was.

"Monica, you alright?" Dante asked as she, Angela, and Geno walked up to him and the others.

"I'm fine!" Monica responded as she hugged Dante's neck. "I know you said to watch her, but she was about to leave Puerto Rico, so I went ahead and—"

"It's cool, Monica," Dante told her calmly before he shifted his eyes toward Angela for a moment.

"Well, I see you're still doing good, Dante. How's our daughter doing?" Angela spoke up first.

"The smart thing to do right now is shut the fuck up,

Angela!" Dante calmly told her, but with a tone that would have spooked anyone else.

"So, you're upset with—!"

"Bitch, you need to shut the fuck up!" Alinna spoke up, cutting off Angela while she stared nastily at her.

"Hello to you, too, Alinna!" Angela said sarcastically before she continued, "Nice black eye!"

Before anyone realized what she was doing, Alinna punched Angela directly in the eye, knocking her straight to the ground.

"Damn!" Maxine said, laughing as she stood looking down at Angela. "I bet you'll be having a better black eye than my girl Alinna now, bitch!"

"Get the fuck up!" Dante told Angela in all seriousness.

James and Monica then snatched her up from the ground.

"Monica, take her to the Range Rover. Greg Wilson will be by the mansion to pick up her and Geno. We'll deal with them later!"

"Dante!" Angela yelled as he turned and escorted Alinna and Yasmine into the back of the Rolls-Royce Phantom.

"Let's go!" Monica said, pushing Angela and Geno toward

the escorting security that stood waiting at the Range Rover.

Once they were all inside and pulled off, Angela called up to Monica.

"So, who's the new Asian woman and where's Natalie, or did she get smart and leave Dante's ass too?"

Monica just turned and gave Angela a nasty look, shaking her head.

"Third wife?" Angela asked, only for Monica to turn back around and ignore her.

* * *

"So what are you planning on doing with Angela, Dante?" Alinna asked him as she sat staring at him as they drove to meet up with his mother, sister, and Dwayne.

Dante remained quiet a moment while he stared out the car window in deep thought.

But after Alinna said his name again, he looked over at her and said, "I don't know yet, Alinna."

"What the hell you mean you don't know?"

"Just that! I don't know!"

"Dante, you playing, right?" Alinna asked while staring at him with a questioning stare.

"Alinna, I know what you want, but this is the mother of my—!"

"I know who the hell she is, Dante!" Alinna yelled, interrupting him. "But I also remember that this is the same bitch who tried to get you the life or death sentence for bullshit! What's not to know, Dante?"

"I tell you what. You deal with her, Alinna! I don't give a fuck what you do to her. I'm just thinking about Mya. Period!" Dante told Alinna as he turned back and stared out the window again.

Alinna stared back at Dante and was unsure whether to be upset with his ass or understand what he was telling her. She was having a hard time because she could only see one ending for the woman who had caused them so many problems.

Once they pulled up to the restaurant with Dante's mother, sister, and Dwayne, Dante was the first one out of the Rolls-Royce. He waited until Yasmine and Alinna got out. James, Gage, and Maxine walked over after climbing out of James's McLaren 650S Spider that was gifted to him by Dante. Dante then led his family into the restaurant and let the hostess know who they were, only to be instantly shown to their table where his mother, sister, and Dwayne were seated. Dante kissed his mother's cheek, earning himself a smile from her.

"Everything okay, sweety?" Brenda asked Dante as the seven of them all sat down.

"Yeah, Momma!" he replied.

"Dante, what's the matter, baby?" Brenda asked again.

"Nothing!" he lied as he picked up a menu.

"Momma Blackwell," Alinna spoke up. "Dante's upset because his daughter's mother is back in Miami and we got into it about a decision he should make but doesn't want to make."

"Let me guess!" Brenda said as she looked at her son. "You're having second thoughts about what you want to do with her now, aren't you, Dante?"

"Yes, ma'am!" Dante answered respectfully. "That's why I told Alinna to deal with her instead of me."

"I think that's a good idea," Brenda stated, looking from Dante to Alinna and asking, "So, what have you decided, Alinna?"

FIFTEEN

Three weeks after returning to Miami, Dante focused his attention on getting business started with Dwayne and the trucking business while Alinna got back to business connecting with the other friends and associates. Dante took a two-day trip out to Orlando to meet with a guy who was selling semi-trucks. He bought tent trucks from the man to go along with the new building that he and Dwayne had picked out.

On the fourth week back home, after getting through the second day of hiring new employees, Dante walked out to his G-Wagen where James and Gage were waiting while Dwayne was walking over to the E-Class Mercedes that was a gift from Dante and Alinna. He climbed in the back of the G-Wagen just as his cell phone went off.

"Food, Gage!" Dante told him as he dug out his phone to see that it was Dre calling. "What's up, fam?" he answered the phone with a smile.

"Fam, you ready to get in some work?" Dre asked Dante. "I know you been out there in Miami laid up living like the king of Miami, but your boy just showed up out here in Jersey and homeboy got some friends with his ass. I'm already dealing with his bullshit now, so what's up? You ready to play, or what?"

"I'm leaving tonight. Meet me at the airstrip in Jersey," Dante told Dre, hanging up the phone immediately afterward and then calling Alinna.

"Hello?"

"Lil' man, where's your mom?" Dante asked, recognizing his son's voice.

"She's right here. Hold on, Daddy!" Dante Jr. told his father.

"Yeah, Dante," Alinna said over the phone after a few moments.

"Alinna, pack me up a bag. I gotta fly out to New Jersey to help Dre out with something."

"Whoa! What's happened, Dante?"

"It's Fish Man," he admitted. "Dre said his ass showed up again, but he supposedly brought a team with him this time!"

"I wanna—!"

"No!" Dante cut off Alinna. "I know what you're about to

ask, but you need to handle shit here, and then you still ain't decided what you're gonna do with Angela. Just let me handle this, and I'll be back afterward."

"Dante, I don't want you out there by yourself. I know you're taking James and Gage with you, right?"

"That's not even a question!" he told Alinna, shifting his eyes back to his boys up front. "Tell Monica I need her to call Nash and tell him I'ma need some toys that'll wake God up in heaven."

"I'll let her know. How long will it be before you get home?"

"Maybe twenty minutes."

"I'll meet you there!"

* * *

Dante reached the mansion sooner than he thought, pulling inside just as Alinna and her security team were pulling inside the gate. Dante climbed from his G-Wagen as Alinna was climbing out of her Wraith. The two entered the mansion behind their son while Yasmine was talking with her Japanese security team.

Dante and Alinna were talking with each other while

walking up the stairs instead of using the elevator. They made it to the bedroom to see both Natalie and Damian asleep in their bed. Dante kissed Natalie awake and let her know what was happening while Alinna was packing him a bag and calling Monica for him.

"My husband," Yasmine called out as she entered the bedroom and got Dante's, Alinna's, and Natalie's attention, "I've spoken with ten of our security men who I've trained myself. They will be going with you to protect you as backup. That is not a request, my husband, but they have their orders and will do whatever is needed to ensure that you're safe and return back to us. Are we clear, my husband?"

Dante was not surprised by Yasmine's protectiveness over him, and he was unable to stop the smile that spread across his lips.

"We're clear, Yasmine!" he replied.

SIXTEEN

D re watched as the G-4 jet landed and rolled to a stop as the hatch opened a few minutes later. Dre broke out in a smile at the sight of his brother once Dante appeared in the door opening of the plane. Dante then looked over to Tony T to see his other brother also smiling at the sight of him standing there.

"He's even brought friends," Tony T stated, seeing James, Gage, and the Japanese security team Yasmine brought. "Those dudes were killing up shit when she sent them with Dante and the others when they got at Garcia Francisco."

"What's good, family?" Dante said as he walked up on and then embraced with Dre and Tony T.

"What's good, family?" Dre replied to him as he and Tony T then embraced with James and Gage.

"So, what's up?" Dante asked, getting straight to the point. "What's the deal on this clown Fish Man?"

"I'ma let Tony T tell you what's up!" Dre told Dante as he pulled out his phone. "I'ma hit up Vanessa and have her send a ride for ya team, since you ain't tell us you was bringing a team."

"Yasmine made me!" Dante admitted. "Matter of fact, tell Vanessa I said to call Harmony because the both of them and the other women need to pack bags because I want all of them down in Miami with Alinna."

"You know Vanessa's not gonna be feeling that, bruh," Dre told him as the line began ringing.

"Tell her I said I'm not asking, Dre!" Dante told his brother, only to receive a nod in response.

Dante turned his attention back to Tony T and stood there and listened with James and Gage as he broke down the news about Fish Man and his so-called crew. He caught Dre's words as he repeated what he told his brother to say.

* * *

Dante saw Vanessa's metallic-gray Mercedes-Benz ML63 AMG as it turned out onto the airstrip, followed by an Escalade truck. Dante put out the Black & Mild he had been smoking as the Benz truck pulled up in front of Dre's H1 Hummer.

"Dante, I am not feeling this shit!" Vanessa told him as she, Harmony, Keisha, and Emmy and the kids climbed from the trucks.

"Vanessa, relax!" Dante told his sister as she angrily walked up on him. "I'm doing this for a reason. Just trust me, a'ight?"

Vanessa sucked her teeth and then rolled her eyes at him.

"Baby, can you grab my bag?" she asked Dre.

"Dante, what's up with Alinna?" Harmony asked.

"She's a'ight!" Dante answered. "But I want you and the others with her while I'm up here. She's holding shit down, but I need y'all to watch her back."

"We got you, boo!" Harmony told him, kissing him on the cheek.

Dante escorted the women to the jet and then waited until the G-4 was in the air. Once again, he and the rest of the Blackwell men climbed into Dre's Hummer while the Japanese men climbed into Vanessa's Benz truck and the Escalade. Within moments, the three vehicles pulled off and headed toward the airstrip's exit.

* * *

Dirt watched the three rides drive away from the airstrip, recognizing Dante Blackwell out of all the men who arrived on the jet. He sat listening to the line ring while continuing to watch the vehicles exit the airstrip.

"Yeah! What's up?"

"Fish Man, this is Dirt!"

"Talk to me!"

"You was right! That nigga Dre called that nigga Dante back out here. It was Dante and about twelve other dudes. But I just saw that tall female and three other women leave on the G-4 Dante just arrived in."

"You say Dante got here with twelve dudes?"

"Yeah!"

"Ain't no bitches come with the nigga?"

"Naw! Just hard legs!"

Fish Man was quiet for a few minutes but then spoke up again and said, "A'ight! Meet me at the airport. We're taking a trip!"

* * *

Dre drove around to some of the spots out in New Jersey, letting the workers see that Dante was back. Dante also stopped by and saw his cousin Floyd and his crew, as well as his sister's boyfriend, Norise, and his team over in Brooklyn and

Manhattan. Dre finally pulled up to the two-story mansion that he and Vanessa found out in Jersey City.

"You say this nigga Fish Man is back and he's got a team, right?" Dante asked as he stepped into the mansion behind Dre.

"Bruh! I already know what you about to say!" Tony T spoke up from behind Dante. "I peeped the same thing. This nigga Fish Man ain't been seen nowhere all day!"

"His fake-ass crew either!" Dre added.

"So have either of you seen this nigga Fish Man since he supposedly got back?" Dante asked.

"Naw!" Both Dre and Tony T answered, but then Dre added, "The young soldier you put in charge of the spot over in Newark said he saw that nigga Fish Man and three other niggas with him."

"And now they're just missing in action, huh?" Dante asked as he sat down on the sofa, sitting back while trying to make sense of what he was hearing. After a moment, he continued: "A'ight. This is what we're doing. Have every soldier and worker we got out here in New Jersey and New York on the lookout for this clown and this team he got. Let them niggas know the first person who finds or sees Fish Man and reports back to me gets $100,000."

"You dead serious, huh?" Dre stated, smiling across at Dante. "For $100,000 you gonna have this fool Fish Man being hunted down like a runaway slave!"

"That's the whole fucking plan!" Dante replied with a smirk.

However, Dante's facial expression quickly changed. "This shit with Fish Man supposed to never went this far! I fault myself for that, so I'ma end this shit now!"

* * *

"Hello!"

"Alinna, it's Diamond, girl! I gotta talk to you!"

"Hey, Diamond. What's up?"

"I know Mr. Dante Blackwell took you back to Miami after what happened, but why aren't you with him now in New Jersey?"

Alinna was caught off guard by what she just heard. She looked over at Yasmine, who sat on her right inside the den at the Miami mansion.

"Diamond, how do you now Dante's in New Jersey?" Alinna asked her.

"Because I just got a call from Kyle, and his ass said he's coming to Miami and wants me to pick him up from the airport."

"How do you know he knows I'm in Miami?"

"Because he told me he has unfinished business with you, and since Dante's out of town in New Jersey, he wants to deal with you now!"

"He said that, huh?" Alinna questioned. "Alright. When is he supposed to be here?"

"Tomorrow morning."

"Alright, here's what I need you to do, Diamond," Alinna told her as she began breaking down her plan to deal with Fish Man's sorry ass.

After hanging up with Diamond once they were finished talking, Alinna looked at Maxine, who stood at the entrance of the den.

"Tell me I wasn't just hearing shit, Alinna! We about to finally dead this fool Fish Man, huh?"

Alinna nodded her head and then began breaking down everything Diamond had just told her about Fish Man. She then broke down her plan for Fish Man's ass.

"So, he knows you're here but doesn't know Diamond works for us, huh?" Maxine asked, just as Rose walked into the den interrupting their conversation.

"I apologize, Alinna, but Vanessa is here and driving up to the house," Rose announced.

"Vanessa?" Alinna repeated as she stood up from the sofa and started out of the den with Yasmine and Maxine behind her as they all headed to the front door.

Alinna unlocked the door and then opened it to see Vanessa, Keisha, Harmony, and Emmy climbing from Dante's G-Wagen. Alinna broke out in a smile when she saw her sisters were actually in Miami.

"Looks like this bitch is happy to see us!" Harmony said jokingly as she and the other women approached the front door.

"What the hell is y'all doing here?" Alinna asked, hugging her girls.

"Your husband sent our asses out here!" Vanessa stated as they entered the mansion.

"Auntie Alinna!" Andre Jr. called out, getting her attention.

"Yeah, baby!" Alinna answered, smiling down at her nephew.

"Where's D.J. and Mya?" he asked her.

"They're upstairs, A.J. Go ahead up to D.J.'s bedroom," Alinna told him, smiling as he took off rushing up the stairs. She turned back to Emmy and said, "Emmy, go ahead on up. Natalie's up there with Damian."

Once Emmy left, Alinna and the women went into the den happy to all be back together minus Amber. Maxine then mentioned that Fish Man was in Miami.

"Wait!" Harmony said, after hearing what Maxine just announced. "What the hell you mean Fish Man is in Miami, when Dante just flew out to New Jersey to deal with his soft ass!"

Alinna spoke up and began first explaining to her girls that she had received a phone call from Diamond. She then discussed a plan she was setting up for Fish Man once he arrived in the morning.

"Girl, you been around Dante's ass too long!" Vanessa told Alinna after hearing what her sister just finished explaining to her and the other girls.

SEVENTEEN

Diamond easily spotted Fish Man as soon as he walked out onto the lobby floor of Miami International Airport, but then she also noticed three guys who were with him. She got control of herself feeling her heart beating fast in nervousness. She then stepped out into the opening, which allowed Fish Man to see her. She also saw the smile that spread across his face at the sight of her.

"What's up, baby?" Fish Man said as he walked up onto Diamond, leaning in to kiss her lips.

"Let's go, nigga!" Diamond told him, holding up her open hand and pushing his face away as she turned and started toward the exit.

"Damn, Fish Man, my nigga!" Ace said with a smile while watching Fish Man's people as she walked away. "Where you find that baby from?"

"I'ma tell you about it later!" Fish Man told his partner while following Diamond outside the airport and into the parking lot over to a pearl white Land Rover Range Rover.

"When you get this?" Fish Man asked once inside the SUV and looking around at the new ride Diamond was pushing.

"Don't get in my shit questioning me, Kyle!" Diamond told him with an attitude. She rolled her eyes at him as she was driving away from the parking spot. "Where am I taking you, nigga?"

"I'm staying with you, but you can drop my niggas off at the Hilton on 7th and 29th Streets," Fish Man told Diamond, only to have her correct his ass.

"First off, nigga. You don't just invite yourself to any fucking place, and I'm not about to drive way the hell across town into the city for your boys you didn't even tell me was coming out with you! But I'll take their asses to the Days Inn over on 199th and 441st Street. Take it or leave it!"

"Whatever, Diamond!" Fish Man replied with a dismissive wave of the hand.

* * *

Diamond arrived at the Days Inn and let Fish Man and his boys head inside to get a room. She rolled her eyes when Fish Man told her not to leave. She quickly pulled out her phone and called Alinna.

"Yeah, Diamond!" Alinna answered.

"Alinna, I'm at the Day's Inn you told me about!" Diamond told Alinna, looking toward the entrance of the hotel. "Fish Man wants to come back to my place though, so he's leaving his people at the hotel."

"That's perfect!" Alinna told Diamond. "Diamond, I want you to do whatever you have to do to get Fish Man tied up, and then go ahead and call me back. I'll be at your place once you call me, alright?"

"Alright! I gotta go! Here he comes!" Diamond quickly told Alinna, hanging up her cell phone right afterward and watching Fish Man walk his lying and trifling ass back out to her SUV.

* * *

After hanging up the phone with Diamond, Alinna smiled at what she heard. She dialed her husband's cell phone number while walking out of her bedroom and heading downstairs.

"Yeah!" Dante answered after the first ring.

"Hey, you! You busy?" Alinna asked as she entered the den and saw her sisters as well as Brenda, Natalie, and Yasmine.

"Naw, shit's dead out here right now! You got everything

under control? You good, right?" he asked.

"I'm fine, Dante. But I need you to come home now. It's very important!"

"What's up, Alinna?" Dante asked, taking on a dead serious tone.

"Dante, just come home!" she told him. "And bring Dre and Tony T with you."

"I'm on my way!"

Alinna heard the call end on Dante's end of the phone. She then lowered the phone from her ear, only to hear Vanessa ask, "What's going on, Alinna?"

Alinna smiled again and told the Blackwell woman everything that was just told to her by Diamond about Fish Man. And what Alinna had to say quickly put a smile on Vanessa's lips as well.

* * *

Diamond crawled out of the bed beside Fish Man when she heard him loudly snoring after giving him the rough sex he loved so much. She snatched up her cell phone and headed into the bathroom, shutting and locking the door behind her. She walked over to the sink and turned on the water, and then she called Alinna's number.

"Yeah, Diamond!"

"Girl, his ass is out like a light! When can you get here?"

"We're already in the area. Do you have him tied up?"

"No! But I can take care of that right now."

"Do it! We'll be there in a few minutes."

After hanging up with Alinna, Diamond shut off the water and went back out into the bedroom to find Fish Man still asleep. She quickly got the handcuffs she kept in the bedside table.

Diamond gently moved Fish Man until he was stretched out on his stomach. She then handcuffed his wrists to the bedpost and then tied his ankles to the bed using a sheet on each leg and around the steel bed frame. Once she was finished, she stepped back and smiled as she looked down at Fish Man stretched out naked across her bed. Diamond then walked over to her dresser and grabbed some underclothes and went to get cleaned up.

* * *

Alinna stared out the back window of the Rolls-Royce Wraith as her chauffeur pulled up in front of Diamond's condo, and saw her Land Rover Range Rover she recently bought.

Alinna waited until the driver opened the car door for her, and then she, Vanessa, and Yasmine climbed from the back of the car.

"Yasmine, have two men come inside with us," Alinna told Yasmine as she and Vanessa started up to the front door to the condo.

Alinna rang the doorbell once at the front door. She looked back to see Yasmine and two of the six guards walking over to the door with them. They waited a moment and heard the door being unlocked and then swung open.

"Everything ready?" Alinna asked.

"His ass is still knocked out!" Diamond told Alinna as she stepped back and allowed Alinna and the others into the condo.

Diamond then locked the door behind them and waved them up the stairs and to her bedroom.

Alinna broke out in a smile as Vanessa and even Yasmine burst out laughing at the sight of Fish Man lying ass-naked on his stomach asleep. Alinna walked over to the bedside, ignoring the sex smell in the air as she pulled out her cell phone and took a picture of Fish Man, which she quickly texted with a message to Dante.

"What are you doing?" Diamond asked Alinna.

"Sending Dante a message," she replied while staring at Fish Man.

She then walked over to the bedside table and reached for the book that sat there, only for Diamond to say, "That's not something you'll be into, Alinna!"

"I'm not looking to read it!" Alinna told her.

Instead, she slowly swung it in the air and slammed the book hard and flat down onto Fish Man's ass.

"Aggghhh!" Fish Man yelled at the top of his lungs, immediately waking straight up out of his sleep.

He then began trying to roll out of bed, only to realize that he couldn't move much.

"What the hell!" he yelled.

"How's it going, Fish Boy?" Alinna spoke up, watching Fish Man's head swing in her direction and seeing his eyes open wide. "Happy to see me, huh?"

"What the hell is going on?" Fish Man asked, but at the sight of Diamond standing with Vanessa and some Asian woman, he knew. "Bitch, you set me up!"

"Yes, I did," Diamond answered with a smile. "I told your

stupid ass I would get you back. You will not play me, you sorry muthafucka! Look at you now!"

Alinna smiled as Fish Man began yelling and trying to get up from the bed. She slammed the book down again and again onto Fish Man's ass until he began pissing on himself.

"Oh hell no!" Diamond yelled when she saw the piss while Vanessa and Yasmine stood laughing at the sight.

* * *

Dante saw his G-Wagen at the airstrip as soon as he got off the G-4 as well as Greg Wilson waiting for him. Dante wasted no time walking right up to Wilson, with James, Gage, Dre, and Tony T alongside him.

"Looks like you're in a rush, so here are the keys and the information you were looking for," Wilson told Dante, handing him the keys and a brown envelope.

Dante thanked Wilson and then tossed the keys over to Gage and made his way to the passenger-side front seat. Once Gage had the engine running and drove off, Dante told him where they were going, after receiving a text message from Alinna. He then turned his attention to the envelope he was just given.

Dante opened up the envelope and pulled out three sheets of paper. He speed-read through the papers and smirked. He then dumped out three photos that were also in the envelope, and actually smiled. Dante put away the papers and envelope, and then pulled out a Black & Mild while already thinking about what Alinna was up to with Fish Man, if in fact it was him in the picture she had sent him.

Dante made the ten-minute drive from the airstrip over to Diamond's condo and saw Alinna's Rolls-Royce and a Range Rover with security on full alert. He quickly relaxed at the sight of the guards. Dante climbed from his G-Wagen with James, Dre, and Tony T following behind while Gage made his way around the SUV and followed.

Dante ignored the doorbell and banged his fist on the front door.

* * *

"That would be Dante!" Alinna said with a smile, after hearing the banging at the front door, which caused Fish Man to really begin trying to get lose. "Diamond, go let Dante in."

Alinna turned her attention back to Fish Man after Diamond rushed from the bedroom. She stood quietly a few minutes staring at Fish Man, until Diamond, Dante, and the rest of the Blackwell men entered the bedroom.

"What the fuck is going on in here?" Tony T asked, with a smirk on his face at the sight of a butt-ass naked Fish Man laid out and tied and cuffed to the bed.

Dante stared hard at Fish Man with a demented smirk on his lips. He walked over and stood behind Alinna, bent down, and kissed her on the neck.

"How long was you planning this?" he asked.

Alinna leaned back against her husband and answered, "Diamond called me as soon as Fish Man called her. I put this together right afterward and then sent you the picture and text message."

Dante looked over at Diamond and met her eyes. He then nodded his head, which caused her to smile.

"Since this is your project, I'ma stand back and let you handle your business, shorty!" Dante said to Alinna.

Alinna smiled and looked over at Vanessa.

"'Nessa! Call the twins, and tell Keisha and Maxine that I got some work for them to do over at Diamond's place."

EIGHTEEN

D ante leaned against the front of Alinna's Rolls-Royce as he watched Alinna exit Diamond's house with Dre, Tony T, James, and Gage all around her. Dante slowly smiled at the simple sight of his wife.

"The fun's over already?" Dante asked Alinna as she walked over to him.

"His ass died!" Alinna told Dante. "Keisha was just getting started peeling the skin off his dick, when his ass died."

"Damn!" Dante said, gripping his manhood and making a face. "Y'all was peeling the skin off that nigga's dick for real?"

"Diamond requested it!" Alinna told Dante, nodding over to Diamond.

Dante looked over to where Diamond stood talking with Vanessa and the twins.

"How you feel about giving Diamond a position with the family? We could use her," Dante asked Alinna.

"I was planning on talking to you about that same thing!" Alinna told Dante, just as their men were carrying out Fish

Man's body and Diamond's bed set.

"Boo," Diamond said as she walked up beside Dante and Alinna, "I almost forgot to tell you, but Fish Man's homeboys are at the Days Inn over on 199th and 441st Street."

"How many?" Dante asked.

"Three!" Diamond told him.

Dante called over James and repeated what Diamond had just told him. He told his brother to meet them back at the mansion after he had handled the three guys.

Dante then looked back at Diamond and asked, "You interested in a position with the family?"

"What?" Diamond cried after what she just heard. "Dante Blackwell, are you serious? Are you offering me a job with the Blackwell family?"

"What do you say, Diamond?" Alinna asked.

"What do I say?" Diamond repeated. "Hell yeah!"

"I'll let you two talk!" Dante told them as he pushed off of the Rolls-Royce. "Alinna, I got something to talk to you about. I'ma be inside your ride waiting."

Alinna watched Dante walk off and then climbed into the back of her SUV.

Diamond shook her head again and looked to Alinna and said, "Damn, that man is just too fine!"

* * *

"What's this?" Alinna asked Dante, after climbing inside the Rolls-Royce and taking the envelope he handed her.

"I had Greg Wilson look up some information for me," Dante told her as he nodded at the envelope. "Open it!"

Alinna looked from her husband down to the envelope she held in her hands. She then glanced back at Dante to see him waiting and watching her. She focused back on the envelope, opened it, and then pulled out the three pieces of paper. As she began reading, her mouth dropped open.

"Dante, where'd you get this from?" Alinna asked, staring at her husband in disbelief.

"I remember the talk we had when we first started kicking it together," Dante told her. "I remembered your mother's name, so I had Wilson do some looking around, and he came up with that!"

"Oh my God!" Alinna said, looking back to the paperwork on her mother and two sisters she didn't even know she had.

"There are pictures inside too," Dante told his wife as he

continued watching her.

Alinna quickly set down the papers and dumped out the pictures. She then broke down as tears began running down her face while she sat staring at the pictures of her mother and sisters.

"They're in Puerto Rico!" Dante announced. "The address is with the paperwork."

"I wanna go see them," Alinna told Dante.

"I know. But what about Angela?" he asked his wife. "What are you gonna do about her, shorty? She's still waiting."

"What do you want me to do with her?" Alinna asked.

"It's your decision, Alinna!"

"But I'm asking you, Dante."

"I've thought about it, and because of Mya, I can't see myself killing Angela. But if she lives, she is to never come back to the United States or I will kill her myself!" Dante said with a sigh.

"What about Geno, Dante?" Alinna asked, after nodding her head in understanding.

"Oh, his ass is dead!" Dante bluntly said, causing Alinna to smile and shake her head.

* * *

After the whole issue with Fish Man and his homeboys was over, both Dante and Alinna dealt with Angela. Dante then had Dre deal with Geno and get rid of the body. Dante left Miami afterward to first fly back to New York with Tony T and Harmony to make sure everything was in order. He and Tony T then made a trip to New Jersey and hooked up with Dre and Floyd to make sure they weren't having any problems and that business was running smoothly.

Dante checked up on Eddie and his cousin Lisa, who was still upset with him. He first spent some time with Eddie, who said he was ready to get back to work. Dante also promised him he would have Tony T call him the next morning about his new shipment as well as have some gunners that would watch his back. Dante then caught up with his cousin in the kitchen. He walked up behind Lisa and wrapped his arms around her. He held her tight enough, but if she wanted, she could have pulled away. But she didn't.

"LaLa, I know I fucked up by not putting men out there with Eddie, and I know I can't take back what happened. But I've never asked anybody for forgiveness before, because I've never had to before. But I'm asking you to forgive me, because now I know a family, and you're a part of it. I understand though if you can't, but I'm still sorry."

Dante released his cousin and turned to walk off. He then started to leave the kitchen, when Lisa cried out his name. He looked back just as his cousin ran straight into him, wrapping her arms around him and crying softly into his chest. Dante spent the rest of the day with Lisa and Eddie, until close to midnight. He then returned to the mansion with Tony T and Harmony right afterward.

Dante crawled tiredly into bed, but called Alinna before going to sleep.

"Hey, baby."

"What's up, shorty? You good?"

"Yes, Dante. You sound tired."

"Pretty much," he answered but then asked, "Where are Natalie and Yasmine?"

"Asleep!" Alinna answered. "So when do you plan on coming home?"

"I gotta handle one last thing, and then I'll be home. So you better be ready to leave when I get there."

"Where we going now, Dante?"

"I wanna meet my mother-in-law and sisters-in-law."

"Dante, are you serious?"

"Just be ready when I get there, shorty."

"I love you so much, Dante!"

"You're my life, Alinna! I love you too, shorty!"

NINETEEN

D ante made it back to Miami early and was met at the airstrip by James and Gage. He then got a few minutes of sleep in the back of the G-Wagen as they drove home. Once he arrived at the mansion, he was met at the front door by Mya, who happily announced his arrival. Dante picked up his growing daughter and carried her into the house, just as everybody started to appear.

"About time you decided—!"

"Ahhhhhh!" Melody screamed, cutting Vanessa off in the middle of what she was saying, after seeing her boyfriend, Norise, standing behind Dante with James and Gage.

She took off rushing toward her man.

Dante stood smiling as he watched his sister and her boyfriend. He then felt arms wrap around him, looking down to see Alinna at his side. He shifted his daughter over to his left side as he wrapped his right arm around his wife.

"You brought him for Melody, didn't you?" Alinna asked him, smiling at her husband.

"You ready to go?" he asked while nodding his head.

"The bags are ready," Alinna told Dante. "I think we should take the kids and both Emmy and Rose with us."

"That's what you want?"

"I want them to meet the rest of their family."

"A'ight! That's what we doing then. Let's get outta here," Dante told Alinna.

He then motioned for the two security men who were flying with them to Puerto Rico to grab the bags that Alinna had set out. They left the mansion a little while later and drove back out to the airstrip. Dante was unable to get a nap this time with Mya sitting in his lap talking to him the entire time. Once they got on the jet, Dante sat with Alinna while Emmy and Rose looked after the children.

"Wake me once we get there!" Dante told Alinna as he then stood up and started walking to the back bed chamber to get some quick and much-needed sleep.

* * *

Alinna enjoyed the flight over to Puerto Rico and woke up Dante once they were descending. She was the first one off the plane, with Dante right behind her. They were followed by

Rose and Emmy and the children being escorted by security. Their Bentley Bentayga and Mercedes GL63 AMG were waiting for them. Dante and Alinna walked over the chauffeur-driven Bentley while Rose, Emmy, and the children were escorted to their Benz SUV.

"Are we going by the penthouse first, or to see my mother?" Alinna asked once she and Dante were inside the Bentley.

"We're already out!" Dante stated as he sat forward to speak with the chauffeur a few moments.

He then sat back beside Alinna, sighing and still a little tired, but feeling better. Alinna didn't bother asking Dante what he discussed with the driver; instead, she leaned back against her husband and relaxed while staring out the backseat window.

Alinna barely remembered any of what she saw as the SUV drove through Puerto Rico. She sat up, however, once the area began to change for the worse and she noticed that the neighborhood was in a poor area by the condition of the homes and streets. She woke up Dante from the sleep he had fallen into, shaking him and calling out to him.

"Huh?" Dante answered, opening his eyes and lifting his head to look over at Alinna. "What's up, shorty?"

"Baby, where are we going?" Alinna asked, looking back out the window.

Dante stared out the window and understood instantly what she was talking about. He saw the area they were driving was an area of Puerto Rico he did not recognize. Dante looked back at Alinna and was bothered by the look on her face. As the Bentley slowed down, Dante looked back out his window as the SUV stopped in front of an old-looking wooden house. He sat staring until the chauffeur opened his door a few minutes later.

"This is the address, sir!" the chauffeur announced to Dante.

Dante climbed from the back of the SUV and then helped Alinna out. He looked back to the Benz SUV and motioned for security to hold off letting out Rose, Emmy, and the kids. He turned back to Alinna and saw her staring at the house. Dante looked to see what had her attention, only to see the same older woman from the photo he gave to Alinna now standing at the front door of the house staring out at them.

"Come in," the woman called to them.

Dante intertwined his hand with Alinna's and led her into the front yard of the house. They started up the dirt walkway onto the wooden porch.

"Can I help you?" the older woman asked in Spanish.

She first looked at the young man, who looked extremely familiar, and then over at the beautiful young woman.

"I-I'm your—" Alinna started, but broke down. She was unable to finish what she was trying to say as tears fell freely from her eyes.

"Ma'am, my name is Dante Blackwell," he introduced himself. "This is my wife Alinna Blackwell. But her birth name is Alinna Rodriguez. She's your daughter, Mrs. Rodriguez."

Mrs. Rodriguez looked at the man whose name she recognized from the news. She then looked over at the young woman, who Dante had told was her daughter.

"Linna, is that really you?" she said in broken English.

Alinna completely broke down and cried harder as she rushed toward her mother. She hugged her, and felt her mother return her hug.

* * *

After introducing themselves to Sophia Rodriguez and allowing Alinna's mother to meet Rose, Emmy, and the kids, both Dante and Alinna sat down. They allowed Mrs. Rodriguez to spoil the children while they all sat talking. Dante then heard the front door open just as two young girls walked into the house.

"Momma, who are all the men outside?" Elayna asked her mother as she and her sister Silvia, entered the house.

"Elayna! Silvia!" Sophia cried happily as she walked over to her daughters and, in English, said, "I want you to meet your big sister and her family."

"Big sister?" both Silvia and Elayna asked at the same time, but froze at the sight of the guy they instantly recognized.

"Momma, that's Dante—Dante Blackwell—from the United States. He's famous," Elayna, the youngest, cried and stared at him.

"He's also your sister's husband," Sophia told her youngest daughter while walking over to Alinna and gently pulling her to her feet. "This is your sister, Alinna Rodriguez Blackwell. Your sister I lost to your father long ago."

"How did she find us?" Silvia asked with a slight attitude

while staring at Alinna.

"I actually had an investigator find you all for Alinna," Dante spoke up, but then surprised them all by saying, "I've actually set things up so you all can come back to the United States and live, so Alinna can be close to you all!"

"Momma!" Elayna cried in shock, rushing to her mother's side. "Can we go?"

"Elayna, we just can't up and go!" Sophia told her youngest daughter. "We have little as it, and then what about Daniel?"

"Mrs. Rodriguez," Dante spoke up, "you don't have to worry about what you have. You're family to my wife, and Alinna needs her family with her. Whoever this Daniel person is, he can come with you if he's important to you."

"Screw Daniel!" Silvia said nastily, just as the front door flew open and an angry, heavy-set guy stepped into the house.

"What the hell are all these guys outside for, Sophia?" Daniel yelled as he suddenly noticed all the people inside the house. "What the hell is going on inside my house?"

"Daniel, this is my daughter and her family," Sophia told her boyfriend while forcing a smile on her face.

Daniel noticed the expression on Alinna's face and even on

the sisters' faces, but he paid close attention to the look on Dante's face. He then aggressively snatched Alinna's mother by the arm and dragged her to the back of the house.

"I hate his ass!" Silvia said angrily after watching her mother allow her supposed boyfriend to drag her out of the room.

"Who's he, Silvia?" Alinna asked as she stared at her sister.

* * *

Sophia Rodriguez was unable to get one word in, and she didn't bother to try either. She waited until her boyfriend finished with his yelling and then she tried explaining: "Daniel, that's my daughter. I—!"

"Shut up!" Daniel yelled as he back-handed Sophia and knocked her to the ground.

Instantly, the bedroom door was kicked open. Daniel spun around to first see the young man from the front room standing in the bedroom doorway. He then stepped aside as the young woman stepped into the bedroom.

"What the hell do you two want?" Daniel screamed.

Alinna ignored Daniel as she walked over to her mother. She squatted down beside her and saw blood on her mother's lip.

"Dante!" Alinna yelled as she looked over at her husband.

Dante heard the command in Alinna's voice and started toward Daniel, who backed up but quickly turned to face him.

"Get back!" Daniel yelled as he took a swing at Dante.

Dante blocked his swing as he connected two blows to Daniel, which caused him to grab his chest. Dante then backhanded the guy down hard to the floor and knocked his ass out.

Alinna watched the entire incident between Dante and Daniel. She then looked back to her mother and met her eyes. "Momma, come back with me, please! I don't want you staying here with him or like this! I'll help you and my sisters!"

"We'll help you, Mrs. Rodriguez!" Dante spoke up as he walked over and helped his wife's mother from the floor.

"Thank you!" Sophia told her daughter's husband with a small smile.

"Momma!" Alinna said, getting her mother's attention again. "So will you come back with us . . .with me?"

Sophia Rodriguez stared into the eyes of her beautiful daughter and nodded her head. "Okay, Alinna! I'll come with you."

"Yes!" both Silvia and Elayna cried excitedly from the bedroom door.

TWENTY

Dante and Alinna stayed in Puerto Rico for a shorter period of time than was originally planned, after getting Sophia Rodriguez and her daughters to move to Miami with them. Dante actually sat back watching Alinna with her family and noticed how fast Silvia took to Dante Jr., after finding out that he was her nephew. He couldn't help but smile when he saw how happy his wife was.

Dante had called back ahead to James to let him know they were coming home, so it was not a surprise to see his G-Wagen, Rolls-Royce, and Bentley waiting with security when they landed. Dante saw James and Gage talking with Yasmine when they all got off the plane. Dante then introduced everyone to each other and quickly caught the way Silvia stared at Gage, who barely noticed her.

Dante left the air strip and headed for the mansion, but made one stop at Elayna's request. She saw the spicy chicken for sale at Popeye's when they drove past, and Yasmine called out and told Dante to stop. He then bought enough food for two families before they finally arrived home at their mansion.

"Oh my God!" both Elayna and Silvia cried out at the same time, once they were standing out in front of the mansion.

"Linna, you all live here?" Sophia asked, staring up in amazement as well.

"Yes, ma'am!" Alinna told her mother. "Come on, and I'll show you around."

Dante smiled while staring and watching Alinna and her family enter the house. He then looked over at Yasmine as she walked up beside him.

"This is nice what you're doing for Alinna, my husband," Yasmine told him, smiling into his eyes.

"I need to be looked after while Alinna is with her mother and sister!" Dante told Yasmine with a smirk. "You feel like showering with me, my wife?"

* * *

Dante allowed Yasmine to have her way, since he was fully aware of how sexual she was and could get. He got her through three orgasms, finally climaxing himself. They both stayed inside the shower a little while longer while discussing a few ideas Yasmine had recently come up with.

"I hope you've got strength for me later!" Natalie said as

she ran into both Dante and Yasmine entering the kitchen while she was walking out. She kissed her husband, but also got a good feel while caressing his manhood.

Dante shook his head as Natalie walked off and headed back onto the patio filled with laughter. He then took the plate Rose had given to him and followed Yasmine outside to see Dante Jr., Mya, and Alinna's sisters in the pool. Alinna, Sophia, Maxine, Natalie, and his mother were all sitting around a poolside table having a conversation.

"Hey, Momma!" Dante said as he walked up to the women's table.

Dante then bent over and kissed his mother on the cheek before he moved over to Alinna and kissed her on the lips.

"Monica wants you to call her!" Alinna then told him.

"About what?" Dante asked, taking the phone Alinna handed to him.

"I don't know," Alinna replied. "She didn't want to tell me."

Alinna watched her husband set down his food and walk off to the side. She then looked at Brenda, who said, "He looks really tired, Alinna. He's been on the go non-stop since coming to New York."

"I've noticed it too!" Alinna stated, looking back over at Dante and seeing how tired he actually did look.

But she also noticed how he still maintained his strong and extremely handsome self.

"Alinna, why don't you and Dante go away for a little while?" Maxine asked her. "Dante does look like he could use the rest."

"That sounds like a good idea, but it will have to wait until I get my mother settled in!" Alinna suggested.

"Alinna, I can take care of getting Sophia settled in," Brenda told her daughter-in-law. "I really think you need to take Dante away for awhile. You don't want him being so tired that when or if something was to happen, he would be useless to the family."

"You're right!" Alinna agreed, looking back over to Dante and noticing the smile he had on his face.

"Alinna!" Yasmine called out.

"Yeah, Yasmine!" she replied, looking over at her husband's third wife.

"I spoke to Dante once before, and I heard him mention he wouldn't mind going to Costa Rica," Yasmine informed.

"Naw!" Maxine spoke up as Melody walked up in mid-conversation.

"Do you all think taking Dante to Costa Rica is a good idea, seeing how he attracts Spanish women and has a thing for Spanish women? Are we looking for wife number four now?" Melody questioned.

"Good point!" Alinna laughed. "Costa Rica is definitely out, but I do know he wants to go to Barbados."

"Who wants to go to Barbados?" Dante asked as he walked back over to the table and caught the end of Alinna's conversation.

"We'll talk about it later!" she told him, picking up her husband's plate of food and handing it to him. "Eat your food!"

* * *

Alinna found Dante lying in bed with Natalie asleep beside him while he watched the news with no volume. Alinna undressed and then put on one of Dante's T-shirts and climbed into bed on his left side, since Yasmine was asleep on his right behind Natalie. She leaned in and kissed his chest and then his lips.

"Sophia and your sisters asleep?" Dante asked as he laid his hand onto the curve of Alinna's ass.

"Yeah!" Alinna answered. "Baby, I've been thinking."

"About what?"

"Remember we talked about going away for a while?"

"Yeah!"

"How about taking a trip to Barbados and just relaxing, just the two of us? You've been running all over the place dealing with so much, and everyone's noticed how tired you look, Dante."

"That sounds like a plan, but I promised Monica I was going to put together a business for her, Nash Johnson, and Greg Wilson. They want to open up an investigation agency, and I believe it'll bring in some good—!"

"Dante!" Alinna cried, cutting him off and getting him to look at her. "Brenda, Yasmine, and, I'm sure, Natalie know the business good enough to take care of all that! So let them take care of it, because we're leaving! I'm not asking either!"

Dante shook his head and began to chuckle.

"I guess we'll see you guys when you get back!" Natalie spoke up.

The End . . .

Text Good2Go at 31996 to receive new release
updates via text message

New book release from J. L. Rose – My Brothers Envy

BOOKS BY GOOD2GO AUTHORS

GOOD 2 GO FILMS PRESENTS

WRONG PLACE WRONG TIME WEB SERIES

**NOW AVAILABLE ON
GOOD2GOFILMS.COM & YOUTUBE
SUBSCRIBE TO THE CHANNEL**

**THE HAND I WAS DEALT WEB SERIES
NOW AVAILABLE ON YOUTUBE!**

**THE HAND I WAS DEALT SEASON TWO
NOW AVAILABLE ON YOUTUBE!**

THE HACKMAN
NOW AVAILABLE ON YOUTUBE!

FILMS

To order books, please fill out the order form below:

To order films please go to **www.good2gofilms.com**

Name:_____

Address:_____

City: _____ State: _____ Zip Code: _____

Phone:_____

Email:_____

Method of Payment: Check   VISA   MASTERCARD

Credit Card#:_____

Name as it appears on card: _____

Signature: _____

Item Name	Price	Qty	Amount
48 Hours to Die – Silk White	$14.99		
A Hustler's Dream - Ernest Morris	$14.99		
A Hustler's Dream 2 - Ernest Morris	$14.99		
Bloody Mayhem Down South	$14.99		
Business Is Business – Silk White	$14.99		
Business Is Business 2 – Silk White	$14.99		
Business Is Business 3 – Silk White	$14.99		
Childhood Sweethearts – Jacob Spears	$14.99		
Childhood Sweethearts 2 – Jacob Spears	$14.99		
Childhood Sweethearts 3 - Jacob Spears	$14.99		
Childhood Sweethearts 4 - Jacob Spears	$14.99		
Connected To The Plug – Dwan Marquis Williams	$14.99		
Flipping Numbers – Ernest Morris	$14.99		
Flipping Numbers 2 – Ernest Morris	$14.99		
He Loves Me, He Loves You Not - Mychea	$14.99		
He Loves Me, He Loves You Not 2 - Mychea	$14.99		
He Loves Me, He Loves You Not 3 - Mychea	$14.99		
He Loves Me, He Loves You Not 4 – Mychea	$14.99		
He Loves Me, He Loves You Not 5 – Mychea	$14.99		
Lord of My Land – Jay Morrison	$14.99		
Lost and Turned Out – Ernest Morris	$14.99		
Married To Da Streets – Silk White	$14.99		
M.E.R.C. - Make Every Rep Count Health and Fitness	$14.99		
My Besties – Asia Hill	$14.99		
My Besties 2 – Asia Hill	$14.99		
My Besties 3 – Asia Hill	$14.99		
My Besties 4 – Asia Hill	$14.99		
My Boyfriend's Wife - Mychea	$14.99		
My Boyfriend's Wife 2 – Mychea	$14.99		
My Brothers Envy – J. L. Rose	$14.99		
Naughty Housewives – Ernest Morris	$14.99		
Naughty Housewives 2 – Ernest Morris	$14.99		
Naughty Housewives 3 – Ernest Morris	$14.99		

Naughty Housewives 4 – Ernest Morris	$14.99		
Never Be The Same – Silk White	$14.99		
Stranded – Silk White	$14.99		
Slumped – Jason Brent	$14.99		
Supreme & Justice – Ernest Morris	$14.99		
Tears of a Hustler - Silk White	$14.99		
Tears of a Hustler 2 - Silk White	$14.99		
Tears of a Hustler 3 - Silk White	$14.99		
Tears of a Hustler 4- Silk White	$14.99		
Tears of a Hustler 5 – Silk White	$14.99		
Tears of a Hustler 6 – Silk White	$14.99		
The Panty Ripper - Reality Way	$14.99		
The Panty Ripper 3 – Reality Way	$14.99		
The Solution – Jay Morrison	$14.99		
The Teflon Queen – Silk White	$14.99		
The Teflon Queen 2 – Silk White	$14.99		
The Teflon Queen 3 – Silk White	$14.99		
The Teflon Queen 4 – Silk White	$14.99		
The Teflon Queen 5 – Silk White	$14.99		
The Teflon Queen 6 - Silk White	$14.99		
The Vacation – Silk White	$14.99		
Tied To A Boss - J.L. Rose	$14.99		
Tied To A Boss 2 - J.L. Rose	$14.99		
Tied To A Boss 3 - J.L. Rose	$14.99		
Tied To A Boss 4 - J.L. Rose	$14.99		
Tied To A Boss 5 - J.L. Rose	$14.99		
Time Is Money - Silk White	$14.99		
Two Mask One Heart – Jacob Spears and Trayvon Jackson	$14.99		
Two Mask One Heart 2 – Jacob Spears and Trayvon Jackson	$14.99		
Two Mask One Heart 3 – Jacob Spears and Trayvon Jackson	$14.99		
Wrong Place Wrong Time	$14.99		
Young Goonz – Reality Way	$14.99		
Subtotal:			
Tax:			
Shipping (Free) U.S. Media Mail:			
Total:			

Make Checks Payable To:
Good2Go Publishing
7311 W Glass Lane,
Laveen, AZ 85339

CPSIA information can be obtained
at www.ICGtesting.com
Printed in the USA
LVOW13s1507260717
542728LV00015B/561/P